BUDDY THE WAR DOG

BUDDY THE WAR DOG

A black Labrador faces the Blitz and
Battlefields of
World War II

by J.A. McEnnis
First published in 2017 by McEnnis Publishing
Wimborne Minster, Dorset, United Kingdom

First published in 2017 © J.A. McEnnis.

Magnolia House
24 West Street
Wimborne Minster
Dorset BH21 1JS

ISBN No: 978-0-9957839-0-4

This is a work of fiction. Any resemblance to persons living or dead is purely coincidental, except in the naming of the Prime Minister and his cat.
Many events described herein are based on actual incidents in World War II although in some cases the author has taken certain liberties with chronology.

Printed by Short Run Press Ltd., Exeter

ACKNOWLEDGEMENTS

Photographs

Braving the Blitz
Front cover - St. Pauls in the Blitz - Imperial War Museum No. HU 036220
Black Labrador - Imagesforall - ID 5871745
Chapter 3. ARP Warden and dog in Blitz - Imperial War Museum - D 005945

Sniffing the Enemy
Chapter 1 - ARP Warden setting blackout clock - Chronicle/Alamy
Chapter 2 - Friend or Foe - radio operator - www.otrcat.com
Chapter 6 - the longest Night - bus in rubble - Imperial War Museum - HU 036188

Invasion of Paris
Chapter 1 - Hitler in Paris Bundesarchiv, Bild 183-H28708 / Photo: Heinrich Hoffmann
Chapter 4 - Convoy - German tanks in forest - Bundesarchiv: Bild:1011-382-0248-33A/ Photo: Böcker
Chapter 5 - Holocaust Train - Holocaust train - first published Poland before 1964 and in public domain on the URAA date (1st January 1996)
Chapter 9 - After the War - "Dig for Victory" poster by Peter Fraser

Called Up
Chapter 2 - Training begins - Dog Detecting mines in France. www.dday-overlord.com
Chapter 3 - The Fearless Four - Parachuting dog - Imperial War Museum - No. EA 000031

Every effort has been made to trace all the photographic copyright holders and obtain permission to reproduce their material. However, in one or two cases where this has not been possible, the author and publisher will be pleased to answer any enquiries relating to the image in question.

I dedicate this book to every brave War dog that has ever lived, past and present who in silent obedience gave their best in the face of danger and fear. Also to Bod (AKA Bees) our family's gentle, funny and playful black Labrador who originally inspired me to write these and other stories.

The stories in this book highlight how dogs were used during World War II (and in wars generally) through the experiences of 'Buddy' - a black Labrador who is requisitioned to serve King and Country. Although this is a work of fiction, the dangers and challenges encountered by Buddy and his canine friends are factual.

Special thanks to my husband, Martin, for his encouragement and enthusiastic support to keep me motivated to finish this book and to my son, Duncan, for his digital advice and expertise. My grateful appreciation to my son Henry and wife Becky and grandson Sennen for bringing Bod (Bees) into our lives. Plus, a big thank you to my friends, Lionel and Deloraine Woodcock for reading my manuscript.

CONTENTS

BRAVING THE BLITZ
10

SNIFFING THE ENEMY
30

INVASION OF PARIS
54

CALLED UP
100

BRAVING THE BLITZ

CHAPTER ONE

GRAMPS WAS MY HERO

Explosive Skies

Archie bounded up the stairs to his bedroom taking two steps at a time. He switched off his light, drew back his curtains, and opened the window.

The still night air hung heavy and hot, charged with pent up energy.
Beads of sweat trickled down Archie's face. And then he heard it; the first distant rumble of thunder.

Hurriedly he assembled his camera on its tripod and fumbled with the settings. "I reckon this is going to be a whopper!" he said nervously to his black Labrador, Bod, who had scampered up after him, panting,whining and agitated. The dog knew that when Archie got his camera out - something was up!

The bad weather warnings along the Cornish coast were usually right and within half an hour a force nine was lashing the Tremayne's clifftop farmhouse. Then a resounding - BOOM! - a deafening clap of thunder shook the windows. "Wow! it's right overhead now. I hope I snapped that fork lightning flash - spectacular!" shouted Archie excitedly.

The storm had woken Archie's mum, Lydia, who did not like storms at all. She ran along the landing and banged loudly on Archie's door. "Are you all right dear?" she said in a shaky, worried voice.

"Just fine Ma. I think I've got some great photos of the lightning."

"Hmm, well I hope your father's okay driving back from Truro in this weather. The roads could be flooded," she said anxiously hurrying back to her room.

"It's a good thing Evie is at her friend's house tonight," mumbled Archie, remembering how nervous his eight year old sister was of storms. 'I bet she's hiding under her duvet!' he thought with a wicked grin.

But meanwhile, Archie and Bod were enjoying the show. In fact, they had a lot in common and liked to talk for hours about life, the universe - and all matters in between.

He knew Bod was a pretty special and brave dog with amazing talents. But what he didn't know was that he had inherited his extraordinary skills from his seven-times-great-grandfather, Buddy.

Archie looked Bod straight in the eye. "I'd like to know how you come to be such a brave dog. You've saved animals and people in your life - including me!"

Bod gave one of his long sighs, held up his right paw and waited hoping for a tasty treat; his way of negotiating a deal you could say.

And once again it worked. He gave a big
doggie stretch and sat upright opposite Archie.

"It comes from Gramps - my seven-times-great-
grandfather," he woofed proudly lifting his
head and looking down his nose at Archie. "His
name was Buddy because he was everybody's
friend and was famous in the War for tracking
the enemy in France, detecting mines and
saving people, just by sniffing them out. He
even helped the police with detective work."

"Wow!" said Archie who was very impressed
indeed. "So he was a hero too? That's so cool!
I'd like to know more about your gramps,"
added Archie with a serious look.

Just then, BANG! the window slammed nearly
breaking the glass. "Phew! better batten down
the hatches!" shouted Archie struggling to pull
it shut.

"Not a good night for a walk so let's go
downstairs and sit by the fire. Then you can
tell me more about your gramps," said Archie.
Together they watched the flames leap and
dance and listened to the logs crackle and hiss.
Bod sat up and began his tale.

CHAPTER TWO

BOMB BLAST

"Did you know Archie that when the War
started in 1939 people were told to kill their
pets to save on food and other trouble? In fact,
in just one week 750,000 animals were put
down. Pets weren't even allowed into air raid
shelters so had to walk the streets where bombs
were falling like rain. So, my gramps, Buddy,
was in great danger!"

"I want to hear everything that happened to
him," said Archie seriously.

"Okay, so here's his story that appeared in the
War Dogs Journal," woofed Bod. "But you'd
better be prepared for some horrible bits," he
added gravely.

Interview by Patsy Carnell - War Dogs Journal

"We know that thousands of canines would like to
hear about Buddy's wartime experiences and how
he escaped being put down like other dogs in the
War," wrote Patsy Carnell, the War Dogs Journal's
editor. "So over to you Buddy for your story."

"Well, It was a dark windy day when my owner, Mr. Crouch, took me into the garden shed and made me lie down. I watched him mix something up in a bowl and just knew it was nasty. Just as he put the bowl down and told me to drink, the air raid sirens went off and the liquid splashed all over the floor. Mr.Crouch shouted out 'No! Edith, Edith!' and ran into the house to get his wife. But suddenly, BOOM! bombs were falling in the street and then - whoosh, bang! one exploded right on our house.

He'd left the shed door open so I dashed out - even though I was scared. I started to run away, but then I heard Mr. Crouch shouting. 'HELP! HELP! Somebody please HELP!'

I had to help them so started digging in the rubble as fast as I could. I howled into the dusty air until two men wearing helmets came, then a lot more. They all started to dig. I showed the men where the right place was but suddenly, the ground began to shake and a loud hissing sound made the men stop.

'GAS, GAS! Back boys - quick!'

'No! Here's a body' said another man. 'Just keep going and pull. Pull - now! ' he screamed.

It was Mr. Crouch. He was holding his wife's hand and wouldn't let go. But then a wall behind them started to creak and shudder. The men scrambled out of the way but I kept pulling at Mr. Crouch's sleeve and barking. He started to crawl backwards slowly holding his wife. Then - CRASH! the wall exploded! Some bits hit them but they kept moving back until the rescue men pulled them free. The first thing he did was stroke my head and say 'Thank you boy for saving us.'

After that, Mr. Crouch gave me to the Air Raid Precaution Wardens (ARPs) as a rescue dog so that I could help to save more people.

'That's amazing!' said Patsy. 'So you became a very precious working dog in the London Blitz and saved lots of people and children?'

I closed my eyes remembering those stressful moments and how sick I felt that thousands of other dogs and cats were put to death. Patsy was gobsmacked! especially when I told her about my girlfriend, Layla, who looked just like me. She was pushed into a 'death truck' to be taken and killed too, but the driver felt sorry for her and secretly took her to Battersea Dogs Home where they looked after her.

CHAPTER THREE

THE SIT-IN

Searching for life in the Blitz

My new master was Sid Malkovich. He was small and thin with spindly legs. He had a little pointy beard and always wore a peak cap as he was going bald. I liked him straight away. Sid was a Jewish refugee from Austria who had to report to the authorities every day. He also had to obey an 8pm to 8am curfew! This was because some refugees were considered suspicious and "unsafe". Like other ARP wardens, Sid was responsible for checking blackout blinds were closed properly on the streets.

On the day the Germans started bombing London in September 1940, I was rushed to a bombed building to sniff out where people were trapped. But sadly, there was no cry for help anymore and when they finally got the husband and wife out, they were both dead. Even so, I kept on digging and barking as I knew there was someone, or something else under the concrete blocks. The rescue men told everyone to stop speaking while they listened. But no sound could be heard. Then someone shone a torch into a small hole in the debris.

'Well I'm blowed! shouted Sid 'It's a dog! Ah well, guess we should just leave him in there - considering that he should be put down anyway,' he told his team. So, they all started walking away.

I barked at them but they weren't stopping - and I wasn't going to leave, so I just kept on woofing, looking into the hole.

Sid shouted: 'Come on now Buddy. We've got people to find. Come 'ere boy - now!'

I didn't look at Sid and refused to move, so he put a lead on me and tried to drag me away, but as I was a very strong Labrador and Sid was only small, he couldn't move me.

'I think he's stagin' a sit in!' said Sid who was amazed - but smiling at my stubbornness. So eventually, he had to give in.

'Okay you wilful old pooch - you win!' he moaned. 'Let's see if we can get that dog out. But I'm not promisin' we can keep 'im - or her - D'ya' understand boy?'

Carefully Sid removed the bricks and rubble to make the hole bigger and then - suddenly - out scrambled a border collie covered in dust and sneezing, but unhurt. Sid wiped the name tag on the dog's collar which read "Peg".

'Well, she's a pretty lady, so I suppose we can keep her for a while,' said Sid stroking Peg gently.

I gave her a big kiss and a nuzzle and Sid

poured some water into my bowl for Peg who was so thirsty she lapped it up in two minutes. It had been a long day so Sid took Peg and me home for some dinner and an early night.

CHAPTER FOUR

DIRECT HIT

German Bombs fall on London

The air raid sirens screamed over the city early next morning as more German war planes headed for London. Ten minutes later Sid's pick-up truck was ready to go, loaded with blankets, water and emergency food and of course - us dogs!

The dusty air smelt of smoke, wet concrete and gas and a thick black dirty cloud hovered over London blocking out the sun. Sid put on his warden's metal helmet and a face mask to keep out the choking air. Through the poisonous smog we heard the muffled wails of fire sirens and ambulances.

Sid made one stop across London to pick up his
friend Alf, another ARP warden. Alf was tall
like a giant and very strong with big muscles
and a hairy chest. He looked fearful but was
really happy and kind. His eyesight wasn't too
good though. That's why he wasn't allowed to
sign up for War service.
He could carry heavy people while little Sid
could creep into small spaces to look for those
who were trapped- so they made a good team.
Peg and I did too. Between us we sniffed
out and saved lots of people and families all
through the Blitz.
Before dawn one morning, the air raid sirens
blasted out across London. We leapt up. In
the rush, Sid fell over his tangled pyjamas -
BANG! - and bruised his arm.

'Quick! let's head for those sirens,' shouted Alf
as he scrambled out of the house and jumped
in the truck still pulling on his clothes. 'Yeah -
that's where we'll be needed,' replied Sid.

Peg and I raced after them and crouched down
in the back of the truck. Black smoke hissed
and belched from the exhaust pipe as it sped
through the bombed streets. The engine roared
so noisily, Sid and Alf didn't hear it at first -

the dreaded engine of the Luftwaffe bomber above the clouds. Peg and I did though. We howled and barked as loud as we could to alert Sid and Alf. Sid braked suddenly and the truck screeched to a halt.

'Quick, get away from the truck and lie flat,' he shouted. 'Roll into that ditch and cover your ears.'

We huddled in the ditch with Sid and Alf. Peg shook with fear, her hackles up. But Sid and Alf held us close with our heads inside their jackets.

The Luftwaffe bomber flew so low Sid shouted: 'Look! I can see the swastika on its rudder!' Then, more planes and the bombs started to fall followed by massive explosions which shook the ground where we huddled. It had made a direct hit in the next street. One of our front tyres blew off scattering rubber bits across the road. We heard screams from the injured through the thick dust and pall of smoke. As quick as lightning, Sid and Alf fitted the spare wheel and soon we were speeding off again heading to the next road. The street was flattened and horrific. Only two houses remained standing. Everywhere else there was fire, smoke and exploding gas from ruptured mains. It was a very dangerous place to be.

We were the first rescue team there. Peg and I had to wear muzzle gas masks against the dust and fumes. We crept forwards very slowly, listening for trapped people. First some taxis pulled up full of sandbags. Their drivers helped and chucked sand onto the fires. Soon afterwards the emergency services arrived and started pulling at the bricks so that Peg and I could get in closer.

We rescued many people that day, but sadly a lot were still missing. It was getting dark and as there were no street lights, rescuers had to work by torchlight. Us dogs became vital to the rescue teams because of our extra sensory sniffing skills.

At first Peg was too scared to go into another hole, as she knew what that felt like. But when I stood by her she felt safe to crawl further in.

CHAPTER FIVE

FIND PEG

It was late in the afternoon when I noticed Peg was missing. I was very anxious so began turning in circles and barking at Sid.
'She can't be too far away,' said Sid patting me on the head. 'She'll be back soon. Don't you worry boy,' he assured.

But after two more hours when Peg hadn't returned Sid and Alf feared the worst. 'She's probably got herself trapped - but where?' said Alf. 'We'll just have to hope she finds her way home.'

Then, walking slowly through the debris, two fire fighters were calling out to the ambulance men. In their arms were two small bodies.

'Over here! Quick men! Two toddlers need oxygen fast. We would have missed them if it wasn't for that collie dog - amazing! What a hero! Trouble is, she's gone back in the building again. We couldn't stop her. She's gone to find the mother I think,' said Joe the fireman.

At that moment, the ground began shaking. 'GET BACK! QUICK BOYS! ' shouted Joe 'The whole upper floor is about to collapse!'

Sid grabbed me and ran fast from the the falling concrete and metal. All the next day bulldozers worked non-stop carefully clearing concrete blocks as big as cars. And all the while I was there waiting for my friend, Peg. I crawled nearer and nearer to the centre of the building and barked and scratched at the ground because I heard something.

Sid raised his hand for the men to stop and listen. They only just about heard a woman's voice crying out deep under the rubble. 'Help, please someone help me!'

Eventually they reached the mother of the two toddlers. Her ankle was trapped under a concrete block, but across her body, keeping her warm was a dusty collie dog who answered to the name of Peg.

'She's stayed with me all night,' sobbed the woman. 'It's a miracle I've survived. The dog kept me warm, but I think she's hurt too!'

The woman, Elsie James and her two toddlers were reunited in hospital with their father. Peg was rushed to the Vet where they looked after her for two weeks. She seemed to make a good recovery, especially when I was by her side. But her big, kind heart had worked so hard and had given so much, it could not give any more.

I cried a lot when Peg died but I visit her grave often and and lie down beside her because that's what friends do and - she was my very best friend."

Awards

Because of their bravery both Peg and Buddy

were officially commended and awarded the animals' Dickin Medal for their gallantry and devotion to duty. Peg received hers posthumously. This award is recognised as the animals' Victoria Cross.

Report by Patsy Carnell - War Dogs Journal

"Well, that's a great story," said Archie to Bod. "Your grandpa was amazing! He'd be very proud of you too Bod if he knew about all the people and animals you'd rescued. And, let's hope you never ever have to go into bombed buildings like your grandpa." Bod looked up into Archie's face, gave him a big doggie kiss - and rolled on his back for a treat and a tickle!

That night, Bod dreamt of his gramps, Buddy, who gave him an important message. "We must not forget what happened then my boy, or how us dogs played a vital part in the War with our extraordinary talents!"

(Next - 'SNIFFING THE ENEMY')

SNIFFING THE ENEMY

CHAPTER ONE

ON A MISSION

Lights out at 5.45pm

"Something extraordinary happened to me in the Blitz in May 1941. It was late one evening when I was out with my master Sid on his walk through the streets of London. As an ARP warden Sid had to check carefully that houses and buildings had their blackout blinds drawn because of the light curfew. Sometimes he'd have to shout 'Switch that light out!' or 'Cover that window!' He was one of 1.4 million ARPs and wore a helmet with a big "W" on the front.

On that night the streets were silent, deserted and very dark. Suddenly my ears began to buzz and I knew I was hearing something strange that Sid, being human, could not hear. I pricked up my ears to listen harder, growled and pulled on my lead. I started to run as fast as I could towards the sound but that made Sid really cross - especially after he fell over - splat! twice.

He was small and not very strong so when he tried to stop me by sitting on the pavement and hanging on to my lead - well, he just bounced along on his bottom! Then his helmet slipped over his nose. I felt sorry for him, but I just couldn't help myself from running. Sid got desperate and shouted out:

'Hey! stop! Heel at once. Slow down Buddy!
right now!'
But shouting was a big mistake as only 200
metres away was a policeman checking for
deserters and enemy aliens. 'Stop! stop! or I'll
arrest you,' yelled the policeman who was hot
on our heels. So I ran faster than ever.

We found a long dark alley. Half way down
were some rubbish boxes where I stopped for
Sid to have a rest and hide. We struggled to
breathe. My pink tongue was hanging out for a
drink but there was no water anywhere.

At the top of the alley the policeman zoomed
past, but then he doubled back and shone his
powerful torch along the alley. We kept very
still, but the light was coming nearer and
nearer. Sid stroked my head as he feared the
worst. Then the policeman's radio walkie-talkie
sounded and he began talking to someone.
Suddenly he turned and walked back onto the
street.

'Phew! that was close boy!' said Sid. 'Perhaps
we'd better just go home now, eh?'

I gave Sid a big kiss but refused to move as my mission was not complete. Slowly we crept back up the alley, listening for danger. The policeman was nowhere to be seen.

Sid was puzzled when I began pulling again for another hundred metres or so until we reached a large white villa off Redcliffe Gardens. I stopped and listened again. There were stone steps leading down to the basement so I pulled Sid down the steps and then pointed my paw up to a little window.

At first, Sid was confused but he then noticed a chink of light in the blackouts. The fan light was open and Sid could hear it as well - a tap, tap, tapping noise and voices. It took him a couple of minutes before he realised the men were talking in German. He crept closer, squinting through the chink in the curtains. Then he saw it! …. a radio transmitter and a hand on the controls - tap…tap…tap..tap. He gasped and nearly lost his balance in shock. 'An enemy agent - at work!' He hissed through his teeth.

CHAPTER TWO

FRIEND OR FOE?

Secret message coming through

It was a still, moonless night and easy to see the flicker of the policeman's torch coming back down the alley.

'Oh no! if he looks down - we're done for!' whispered Sid anxiously. Suddenly the torch went out so Sid braved it up the steps to street level and peeped through the railings.

The policeman had stopped to tie up his bootlaces. Sid noticed that the next door basement had a tarpaulin covering something and there was a big gap behind it where we could hide.

'Quick boy, run! Let's go next door. It's a safer hiding place.' We just made it in time and huddled down behind two bicycles under the tarpaulin.

The policeman's boots clumped loudly on the pavement. Sid held his breath as he got closer and closer. When he was right above us, Sid was just about to go up and reveal what he had seen when we heard the policeman going down the steps next door where we had been! He gave a special tap on the door - TAP-TAP, TAP TAP TAP! The door creaked open and the two men greeted each other in low voices, 'Guten abend Herr Brauer,' said the policeman 'Willkommen Herr Schulz' replied the radio man.

Sid moved quietly back up the steps to listen. He was shocked when he heard the policeman talking to the other man in German before going inside. They became more friendly and used their first names, so Sid knew the radio man was Klaus Brauer and the policeman - Gerhard Schulz.

Sid scratched his head, thinking what to do. He was very worried. 'This is a serious situation. I have to tell someone. Let's go boy - quickly!' he stammered. I scampered up the steps. But in his rush to follow, Sid's coat caught on a bicycle and sent it crashing down - BANG!

'Run, run boy. Don't stop!' Being totally black, I faded into the night and disappeared into the darkness. Next door, Sid heard the door creak open and voices of the men. They had heard the noise and were coming to investigate. But they switched to speaking in English.

'What the hell was that?' said the policeman Gerhard Schulz who had his torch aimed at Sid. Afraid he was about to be busted Sid froze. But just as he was about to surrender, a better plan popped into his head. 'Desperate times call for desperate measures,' he told himself.
He flopped down halfway up the steps mumbling and after a loud belch blurted out.

'Beg pardon! It's me wife's potato wine ye see - gone to me 'ed. Ooops! Don't let zeee ol' dragon catch me or she'll do me in mate!' And after a long fart he started to giggle - as did the policeman and the secret agent.

The policeman didn't know what to do so helped him to his feet. 'You'd better get home to the dragon - or do you want me to lock you up?' Sid's heart was pounding, but he kept his nerve. 'Hmmmm, oooo no! I'd better face the ol' dragon for me sins s'pose, s'pose. Ooops.' Another loud burp and he staggered off into the darkness like a good drunkard, proud of himself for tricking the traitor policeman.

When Sid was out of sight of the men he ran the rest of the way home. I was there waiting, snoozing on the mat under the porch. Sid was totally proud of me though tracking down the radio transmitter. He wanted to tell the authorities immediately, but it was far too risky to go out again that night.

CHAPTER THREE

DISGUISE

A watery sun hung over the devastated bombed streets of London. This made Sid realise it was only going to get worse. So, we hurriedly prepared for our mission - to expose the two traitors!

The wardens' head quarters had been set up in the basement of the council offices in Westminster. It was a gloomy basement room, a bit like a bunker, with gloss painted walls, half white and half green with a brown horizontal line dividing the colours. The only natural light peeped through two long windows about 6 mtrs long x 40 cms high which were up at ground level. Grass and weeds regularly grew over the yellow, dirty glass, sometimes covering the plastic ventilation window vents. This made the room very stuffy, especially with the smell of stale cigarettes. Inside there were trestle tables for desks piled high with files around typewriters.

When we walked in, Sid had the worst shock ever! Sitting at the top boss's table was the 'policeman' we had seen the previous night - but now disguised as an official warden and the very person Sid had planned to expose! They called him Mr. Brown and all the other wardens - at least 60 of them - were taking orders from him and making him cups of tea. He was tall and fat with a big brown curled up moustache, a bit like a circus entertainer. And he had a very loud gruff voice.

Sid panicked and turned to leave but Mr. Brown had seen him.

'Hey! you!' he shouted 'report your case here!' Sid's legs went weak and wobbly as he was scared in case Mr. Brown recognised him. I sensed Sid was afraid and had to help him, so I caused a big rumpus. I barked, whined and woofed and ran out of the door pulling Sid behind me up the stairs and out into the street.

'Next!' shouted Mr. Brown who didn't really care who he saw, except if they had special info he could use to his own advantage.

'Phew! that was a lucky escape,' Sid said. 'Thanks mate you saved me back there. I don't think he recognised me from last night - but

I'm not sure,' he said with a worried look. Sid wondered what to do next as he didn't know who to trust with his story. Also, time was running out if the Germans were planning another big attack on London.

It was by chance we passed a news vendor further down Whitehall shouting the newspaper headlines: 'Read all about it -The Prime Minister Winston Churchill in emergency talks tomorrow.' It was Thursday 8th May, 1941.

Sid rushed to buy a newspaper. 'That's it!' he shouted punching the air. 'I've thought of a plan! But it's very daring.' Sid stopped and looked out over the bombed streets of London. 'There's just no choice boy - I've got to give it a go.'

We ran home fast. Immediately Sid sat down and wrote a letter. It was addressed to The Prime Minister, Winston Churchill and marked URGENT - TOP SECRET - 'Strictly private and confidential'. In it he explained what he had seen and heard about Gerhard Schulz (aka Mr. Brown) and gave the address of the basement flat. Also, he understood that the next air raid was to take place:'Am morgen des 10.

Mai- Raid von der Luftwaffe' which meant the Luftwaffe were planning another air strike on London on 10th May.

The problem was, how could he deliver the letter direct to the Prime Minister? Would the police believe him or could they be trusted to deliver it? It was all too hit and miss. So Sid decided he had to find another way.

CHAPTER FOUR

A DARING RISK

'You're the only one I can trust matey,' Sid told me stroking my head. 'I'll put the letter in a small bag and tie it to your collar. Then, somehow, we have to think of a way of getting you into No.10 so that Winston can find the letter.'

Well, I was always up for a challenge and didn't want to let Sid down but I was scared as I was only a dog in the War and could easily get shot or caught and put down. I had to stay brave.

Early next morning, Thursday 8th May, we arrived in Whitehall close to No.10 as no one knew what time the generals and probably M15 were arriving. We waited for three hours! until 10.30am. Then three black limousines turned into Downing Street. It was easy to get close as there wasn't a lot of security.

Well, what happened next was unreal! The sky darkened from pewter to black. Storm clouds rolled in followed by loud claps of thunder.

Then, tendrils of lightning hit the Thames and the clouds exploded throwing giant hailstones all over the streets. It was like a tornado! During the pandemonium Sid seized his chance to set me free. Nobody noticed a black Labrador sneak through the legs of people rushing out of limousines and into No.10.

But my entrance into the house turned into a very painful experience!

Stretched out on a Persian rug in the hall was Jock, Winston's favourite marmalade cat. Jock's green eyes widened when he saw me. He shot up in the air, back arched, tail up - hissing and showing his fangs and with one enormous leap flew at my throat, claws out.

Jock sank his sharp teeth into the side of my throat. I howled out in pain. Luckily though, my big fluorescent 'Rescue Dog' collar saved me from having my tonsils ripped out by Jock. By the time the butler reached me and Jock, I had shaken myself free and darted out of the house at great speed.

I ran back fast to Sid who was most distressed. There were teeth marks and blood on my collar and the letter was missing - apart from a fragment of paper caught under my collar.

Sid let me splash in a big puddle for a drink followed by another two treats. My neck wound wasn't serious but Sid decided we should go home and bathe it, just in case.

Inside No.10 Jock had scarpered upstairs with the letter in his mouth and crept under a chair in the Prime Minister's bedroom. When he returned downstairs a few hours later, Jock was congratulated on his defence efforts by Winston and the household.

'Jock fought like a lion Sir,' said Max the butler. But Winston was puzzled.
'Must have been that storm that sent the animals loopy. I'd like to know where that Labrador came from. The poor animal must have come off worst under Jock's claws. Most odd, most odd,' he said puffing intently on his cigar.

The next morning, the housemaid, Molly, was cleaning the bedrooms when she moved the chair in Winston's room to vacuum the carpet. She stopped just in time before the letter got sucked up in the rotating brushes.

'Now, what's this piece of rubbish doin' 'ere?' she mumbled to herself. Although the envelope was badly torn, she could still make out the words "TOP SECRET". She gasped and her hand trembled when she looked at the writing closer and the word '-- RGENT". 'S'pose that's "URGENT"! Oh my word. Better take it to the master straight away!'

'Sir is not here and I cannot disturb him as he's with MI5 and his generals until late afternoon,' said Max the butler looking down his long, curved nose at Molly. 'It looks like a chewed piece of rubbish only good for the bin I'd say. Just chuck it please. He's not to be disturbed.' Molly nodded, put the envelope in her apron pocket and went back to her cleaning. But she didn't throw the letter away. Instead, she left it on the Prime Minister's dresser.

CHAPTER FIVE

SHOOT OUT

The next day was Friday 9th May, so it was absolutely crucial that M15 and the armed forces knew what the letter said, as something was definitely going to happen on 10th May according to what Sid had heard.

Late that afternoon on 9th May, Molly made sure she was around when Winston retired to his study on the ground floor. The butler was talking in the kitchen so she only had minutes to get Winston's attention. She knocked quietly on the study door, but there was no response. Her nerves began to fail and her palms were sweating, as if Max saw her, she'd be severely told off and maybe even sacked.

She heard Max's voice talking to the cook in the kitchen as he began to move towards the corridor. Panic stricken, she knocked louder, but still no answer. She was about to turn away when the door began to open. A puff of cigar smoke drifted out and nearly made her cough as Winston stood in the doorway holding Jock his cat.

He was astonished to see Molly and frowned at being disturbed, but sensing her anxiety, smiled faintly. But just then the butler arrived and was angry. 'I'll take it from here Miss. You can go now.' She was about to turn when the Prime Minister said: 'Have you something to say Molly?' 'Er, beg-your-pardon Sir, er yes,' she replied timidly

'Well, you'd better come in then lass,' replied Winston as he shut the door leaving Max gobsmacked and even more angry. Molly explained where she had put the letter and how it looked important.

'We'd better go and have a look at it straight away then,' said Winston in a kindly voice. Much to the dismay of Max, Molly followed Winston up the stairs. She waited outside his bedroom while he went in and got the letter. 'Oh dear, it is in a state,' he said as he carefully opened it. On reading its contents, he stubbed out his cigar and held his hand to his head. 'This could be very serious indeed. Thank you Molly.'

Feeling a bit more relaxed, Molly said she

thought the dog had brought it in but that the cat had torn it from his collar.

'Ha! well I'm blowed!' exclaimed Winston. 'That's too amazing for words. I must meet that dog and his owner! But now let's get moving. Thank you again Molly - and - well done lass.' Winston Churchill summoned his Parliamentary Private Secretary (PPS). 'Put everything on hold and cancel all my appointments,' he ordered. 'And contact the Generals and MI5 immediately!'

Soon, the Secret Intelligence Service (SIS) were sent to the house off Redcliffe Gardens. Heavily armed they first knocked unsuspiciously on the door. It creaked open.

'Yes, can I 'elp ya,' said the landlady in a gravelly voice.

'We've come to see Klaus Brauer,' replied the SIS officer in a quiet, strong voice.

'Ah, well - er - 'e ain't 'ere,' answered the woman nervously.

'We know he is,' insisted the officer and flashed his identity card as they pushed past her into the house and quietly crept up the scruffy wooden stairs to Brauer's room on the top floor. They knocked gently on the door. There was no answer. After the third time, an officer shouted: 'Come out Brauer - now! or we're coming in!' No response, so three SIS officers started to kick at the door. They jumped back as - BANG! BANG! BANG! - three shots were fired at the door from inside the room.

'Ahhhh!' shouted one of the SIS men. He dropped to the floor holding his arm and moaning. Blood was pumping out of his jacket.

'Shoot the lock,' demanded Bill another SIS officer. The door swung open and the men stood aside. 'Come out with your arms up or you'll be shot!' yelled Bill. But everything was silent. Bill placed his helmet on the end of his gun and moved it over the open door space. BANG! rat-a-tat-tat BANG! two bullets hit the helmet. Bravely another officer jumped into the room gun cocked towards the direction of the fire. Lying on the floor furiously reloading his pistol was Klaus Brauer. But too late. 'Drop it or I'll fire!' said the officer who wanted to capture Brauer alive for questioning. 'NEIN! - dummkopf Englander!' retaliated the German. Seconds before he put the gun to his own head four SIS officers pounced and cuffed him.

Back at the wardens' head quarters at the council offices, the building was sealed off and Mr. Brown (aka Gerhard Schulz) was captured for questioning. At his home they found a detailed German plan of attack by the Luftwaffe on London to take place on the night of Saturday 10th May 1941 - exactly one year after Winston Churchill became Prime Minister on 10th May,1940.

CHAPTER SIX

'THE LONGEST NIGHT'

Bus destroyed in the Blitz

Radio programmes across the country were interrupted and people were advised to leave London immediately if they could. If not they should go straight to any one of the eight deep-level air raid shelters beneath the underground stations and take with them warm clothing, food and water. Extra train and coach services to special destinations were put on for the overnight evacuation and all hospitals and emergency services in London and beyond were put on high alert.

The long howl of air raid sirens sounded at 11pm on Saturday10th May when the Luftwaffe started to bomb London. People said it was the worst night of the Blitz - the longest night - which went on until about 5.30am the next day.

Nearly 1,500 people were killed in London as well as hundreds of fire fighters. Over 11,000 houses were flattened and many of London's important buildings were hit including the Houses of Parliament, Waterloo Station and the British Museum. It was recorded that: 'over 700 tons of high explosive and 86,000 incendiaries were dropped across London.' Winston Churchill kindly arranged for Sid and me to be taken to a safe shelter - so we survived the night. During the next day we helped to rescue more trapped people.

The Prime Minister was very grateful to Sid and especially, he said, to me for finding the enemy agents! He said we helped to save hundreds, maybe thousands of lives. After that I was nicknamed 'Sniffer Agent No. 1' due to my talents for sniffing and hearing danger. Sid and I were given a special pass to 10 Downing Street so that if we ever sniffed out anything else we could report it straight away directly to the PM. Even Jock the PM's cat decided to be friends with me - but on one condition - that I didn't try to sit on Winston's lap!

We didn't know that big changes were happening abroad until two weeks later when Sid received a very troubling letter from Paris and meant we would definitely need to use our special Pass to 10 Downing Street!**"**

(Eight months earlier starting on 7th September 1940, London was bombed by the Luftwaffe for 57 consecutive nights. More than one million London houses were destroyed or damaged, and more than 40,000 civilians were killed, almost half of them in London.)

(Next - INVASION OF PARIS)

INVASION OF PARIS

CHAPTER ONE

THE LETTER

Hitler arrives in Paris 1940

"The letterbox snapped shut and made me jump! I was snoozing and enjoying the morning sun streaming through the lounge window and into my basket. I dashed to the front door barking loudly.

A thin airmail envelope lay on the floor. I sniffed it and backed away fast. The scent definitely meant trouble! Very carefully, I manoeuvred it into my mouth and crept upstairs to find Sid.

The bathroom door was ajar so I sneaked in. Sid was shaving with his cut-throat razor and humming a song. He didn't hear the door open with the water running so I gave his leg a big nudge.

'OUCH! What the blazes? What you up to boy? Now I've nicked myself. Could have cut my throat!' he muttered crossly. He was about to scold me but then noticed the letter in my mouth.

'Now, you ain't done that before boy, so what's all this about eh?' I looked up at Sid and gave a big sigh. "Well, go on then - open it up. It looks important!" I woofed.

Sid took the letter into his bedroom and drew the blackout curtains wide. Sunlight lit up the dimly decorated room showing up its faded wallpaper and dark brown doors and skirting boards.

'Well, it's a gorgeous day, so maybe this is a good news letter,' smiled Sid. He looked closely at the French stamp and handwriting. 'Ah! must be from my daughter, Ruth in Paris,' he said happily. 'Haven't heard from her in a while with news of my lovely granddaughter, Meira.' But then Sid noticed the postmark - it was nearly two weeks old - dated 20th August, 1941.

'This wretched War. Can't rely on anything arriving on time these days,' he moaned.

I put my paw on Sid's knee to comfort him as I knew something was not quite right with the letter, even before Sid opened it.

Sid started to read out loud, as he knew I understood every word! I cocked my ears and listened intently. 'You and I are both worried now boy,' he said stroking my face gently.

"Dearest Pa, I hope you get this letter which I am sending via a friend who is hoping to get to Switzerland. The news from Paris is not good. Everywhere is dire madness with people trying to escape, including non French refugees from Holland and Belgium. Even the British and US Embassies are more-or-less closed. I've heard the Nazis are stopping trains and boats leaving France. Some trains are even being bombed if they don't stop! They are looking for Jews, in particular. We've heard Jewish men are being rounded up like cattle and being loaded onto cargo wagons going - who knows where?

We are trying to leave - if we can get through - just after we've secured our valuables to collect later. No time to linger now, except to say - any help you can give will be most welcome! If and when we reach England I'll get in touch straight away.
Your ever loving Ruth, Abe and little Meira."

Sid had heard the rumours about the Jews, but now the truth of it shocked him to the point of rage and tears. He, Ruth, Abe and Meira were Jewish. Abe's name, Grundman, was a dead giveaway Sid told me, as was his - Malkovich. The thought of Ruth and Meira coming to harm was just too much to bear for Sid.

He stroked my upturned head and said 'So, that's no news in two weeks since they wrote this letter. I should have heard something by now.' Dark thoughts filled Sid's mind and his eyes were filled with tears. I grunted and whined a bit then paced around the room looking for a solution. I stopped at the side table and looked up at a photograph of the Prime Minister Winston Churchill with all his medals. 'Perhaps he can help,' I thought and waved my paw in the air. At that very moment, Sid found hope.

'That's it! boy. Well done!' shouted Sid. It was 10.30am and Sid decided he couldn't waste another precious moment. 'We have to head for Downing Street straight away with our special Pass to the Prime Minster's office!' he shouted excitedly. The Pass was awarded to Sid and me after our amazing spy detection work which had saved hundreds of lives in London. So now, Sid reckoned it was time to call in a favour.

CHAPTER TWO

BARRED

Sid felt lucky and honoured to have friends in high places - even confident that somehow he'd be able to help Ruth, Abe and his lovely granddaughter to get home.

Sid was small and thin so I, being a strong black Labrador, found it easy to pull Sid along very fast indeed. In fact, I knew the streets of London better than any London cabbie so could easily sniff out the shortcuts through winding back streets and alleyways.

Ten minutes later, we rounded a corner into Downing Street. But I noticed something was different. I stopped and barked up at Sid. He felt it too and for a while we were doubtful. Two brawny, tall security guards were standing outside the front door of No. 10.
'Haven't seen them before,' Sid mumbled with a puzzled frown. They looked fierce and unfriendly. Not at all like the other ones we had helped to find the spies. 'Well, we have our Passes, so let's go boy.' said Sid cheerfully. But when the guards saw us they braced their big

muscly shoulders and grunted in a menacing way.

'STOP! exactly where you are. You're not allowed here so be off with you! growled the larger of the two men. He took out a truncheon and waved it about in a threatening way. I sensed Sid was very nervous and could hardly speak. I sat up straight glaring at the men, ready to pounce should they dare to hurt my best friend.

'Well, I've got this see,' Sid stammered, holding up the Pass which had been awarded to us by MI5 and which said SPA (short for Special Agent) No. 2 followed by a long number. Gus, the big guard strode towards him with a nasty attitude and snatched it from Sid's shaking hand. I growled loudly which made the guard back off a little. After all, he didn't want an incident outside No.10 on his watch. He looked at the Pass, turning it over and holding it up to the light. He then looked Sid up and down sneering at his scruffy appearance. Sid wore a peak cap, a collarless shirt and a worn out brown jacket with a button missing. His old grey trousers were stained in places with mud from walking me in the rain and around bomb sites. What's more, the sticking paster on his chin from his shaving nick made him look even scruffier.

'Have you stolen this document?' questioned the guard, his steely cold blue eyes narrowing to slits. Sid flinched, his heart pounding with anger. But he knew he had to keep his cool. 'Er, no sir, course not. It's my Pass to see the PM. He gave it to me - er, to us, my dog and me, after we helped him find traitors hiding in a flat.'

'Oooooh, get you! D'ya hear that Jim?' he sniggered as he turned to his companion. 'He reckons he's good at OUR work! Ha, ha!' The men spitefully enjoyed the joke for a few minutes, waving Sid's Pass in the air as if it was worthless.

'It's a windy day. It might just blow away out of my hand. Ooops! and there it goes....' He released the Pass which fluttered to the ground and was soon swept along the street heading for the road.

Being an ace chaser of anything that moves I bounded after it - but straight into on-coming traffic. I heard a screeching of brakes and smelt rubber burning as the Austin 8 hit and mounted the pavement.

Sid screamed: 'Oh NO, NO, my dog. OH no.' The guard rushed over. The driver of the car was shaking and his car was a wreck! with damaged suspension and its exhaust hanging down.

But all Sid was concerned about was me. He anxiously looked around shouting my name over and over again. 'BUDDY, BUDDY where are you Buddy?' I managed a muffled howl. I felt dizzy. My back leg was hurting but I could still wobble about with three, so I hopped slowly back to No. 10 with the Pass in my mouth - shaking and limping but in one piece. Sid raced over to me outside the famous black door. It opened slowly and there stood Max the butler who had heard the commotion.

Gus the guard was fuming as he raced over. 'Get that bloody animal away from 'ere. All this is his fault! Go on, clear off - or I'll kick you to Timbuktoo!' he bellowed throwing his arms into the air. The fact that the guard had caused the incident in the first place by chucking away Sid's Pass did not bother him one bit.

A police car and ambulance with sirens blasting screeched to a halt. Two officers leapt out and ran to the driver of the car who fortunately was not hurt.

Meanwhile, we stood in the doorway of No.10. Standing looking back at us with astonishment were Max and Molly the maid who were very pleased to see us and invited us into the kitchen to recover with tea for Sid and a big bowl of water for me.

The guards were gob-smacked, scratching their heads, frowning and trying to make sense of it all.
'Well, we was only doing our jobs mate,' Jim muttered to Gus. 'How's we to know about them there Passes?' he added sheepishly.

In the kitchen Sid wasted no time explaining to Molly how his sister and her husband had gone missing and what was happening in Paris with the jews.

'I've got to get over there and see if I can

track them down,' said Sid with his head in his hands. 'She's the only family I've got left now,' he whispered wiping a tear from his cheek.

'Well you stay here until the PM returns. He'll know what to do. You'll see,' said Molly in a comforting way.

Later, when Winston and his PPS returned they had already been briefed about the incident with the guards, so were keen to find out exactly what Sid really wanted. After reading his daughter's letter, it was clear to the Prime Minister why Sid wanted to help her but his advice was troubling.

'We can fix you up with false papers so that your Jewish name is changed and can get you across the Channel, but from thereon - no guarantees. You're on your own. We've got contacts with the Resistance who may be able to help. Good luck my man. Keep safe.'

CHAPTER THREE

THE TUNNEL

Two days later, via special messenger service from M15, Sid received a package containing his new identity papers: a new passport, birth certificate and other documents which he might be asked for such as his revamped electrician qualifications bearing his new name - Sidney Butler

The following night, Sid and I travelled to Dover by train, then by ferry to Calais. We were given instructions to go to the Cafe Rennes and ask for Gerard.
The streets of Calais were restless with people hurrying about, some on cycles, some on motorcycles piled high with bundles.
When we got to the cafe it was crowded with French, Belgian and Dutch refugees with their suitcases. Everyone was trying to find a passage to either England or America on any sort of boat that was going.

When Sid ordered a soup and coffee and said "Gerard," we were taken to a small table at the side of the bar where we waited for over two hours. I lay at Sid's feet and had a snooze.

Eventually, the bill was brought to Sid on a saucer, but when he opened it, it said in English: 'Go to back'. Sid hoped it meant - go to the back of the cafe and not 'go back to England!' He waited a few minutes then we walked slowly through to the back of the room which was large and smoky with the pungent smell of Gauloise cigarettes. He pushed through a beaded curtain where he found three green painted doors.

'Which one Buddy?' he asked me. After a few sniffs I chose the middle one which opened into a long, dimly lit corridor with lots of photographs on the wall of entertainers and circus type people. There was a strong smell of fermenting wine and garlic being cooked which made us feel hungry!

Somebody whistled. I stopped and looked up at Sid feeling worried but Sid stroked my head reassuringly. 'It's okay boy. It's okay.' But in fact, Sid was far from happy. In fact, I sensed he felt very uneasy indeed. We followed the corridor round two corners, then down some stone steps. At the bottom there was another heavy, scruffy looking wooden door. Sid tried to push it open but it was locked, so he knocked gently at first and then loudly.

He was about to turn and walk back up the stairs when, suddenly, the door swung open and there stood a pretty young woman with long dark hair and green twinkling eyes. Her dazzling white smile was welcoming and kind and soon Sid was smiling too. She spoke first in broken English. Her voice was soft and comforting.

'You 'ave come a long way I theenk, yes?' She held out her hand in welcome. 'You can call me Fleur,' she said as she led us through the door into a small room stored with boxes, chairs and old chests.There were no windows. Just one dangling electric bulb. It looked spooky and uncared for.

I felt excited and sniffed around the room which had heavy flagstones on the floor. At the far corner were some cardboard boxes piled around a heavy steel chest. I could smell and hear something very strange on the floor.

'Ah, he is very good I theenk,' she said giggling and gave a little clap. I tipped my head on one side to listen. A scuffling noise was coming from under the floor. I backed off quickly, woofing. It was my way of saying to Sid 'Found something here!'

A few minutes passed, then very slowly the boxes began to move. Fleur whistled through two fingers and that's when the boxes started to move faster and the lid of the big steel trunk began to lift up. My ears flattened and I looked up at Sid to make sure he was all right with this game.

First a man's head with lots of curly brown dusty looking hair and a tanned face popped up. He looked as if he'd had flour tipped all over him. Fleur giggled. 'Ah, thees is Pierre, mon frère, er, my brother,' she said. Soon Sid was laughing too. I tried to scramble over the boxes to reach Pierre to greet him but got stuck half way. Pierre laughed some more and patted my head.

'You 'ave to come with me quickly Monsieur Sid,' said Pierre in a deep, gruff voice. Very soon Fleur and Sid were moving the boxes around so that Sid and I could reach the trunk. Then suddenly, Fleur raised her hand 'Sssh, we must be very quiet and 'urry. It is not safe 'ere. We trust no one!'

Sid was amazed to see the trunk had a false bottom which fell down through a trap door under a flagstone into a room. A ladder was propped up against it. Fleur found a big old blanket to wrap me in. 'We shall lower you down in thees cloth,' she whispered.

It was pitch black. Pierre switched on his torch. We were standing in another long passageway which twisted and turned through more tunnels. After about fifteen minutes in the labrynth, Sid lost his sense of direction completely. Suddenly, we reached a huge underground cellar which was stashed with old wines.
'We 'ope the Nazis will not find our wines 'ere!' chuckled Pierre, wiping flour from his face. 'Ha, ha! if they stop to dreenk it - then they will not find their way oot! ha!, ha!' he laughed.

Further on through the tunnels, Pierre stopped in front of a big wooden vat which smelt of fermenting wine. He carefully felt around the edge of the rim and pressed. The front of the vat loosened and slowly Pierre pulled it down.

It was empty. He walked inside and once again pressed on the back rim. The back was a door which opened out into a black cavity beyond.

CHAPTER FOUR

CONVOY

German tanks in the forest

'Come, quickly thees way!' he beckoned. Then Pierre dropped down onto soft earth. The other side of the vat was built into a stone wall. After sealing the vat again Pierre shone his torch around us. We were standing in a field at the back of an old church. It was nearly midnight. The air was scented with wild flowers drifting on a gentle breeze through the tall poplars and grasses. All was silent, except for the sounds of crickets and toads. I was so pleased to be back

in the fresh air and enjoyed a long drink from a
horse trough.

'Now we must wait until the farm truck comes
for us,' said Pierre giving a big yawn. We were
all tired and hungry but had to listen out for the
farmer who we hoped was on his way. After
two hours both Sid and Pierre had fallen asleep.
It was a starlit night and the fields were bathed
in a steely blue moon glow. But something
was happening. The sky became brighter and I
could hear a strange noise. I grunted and licked
Sid's face to wake him.

We crouched under the poplar trees. Sid fixed
my collar and lead and held me tight 'Ah, we
must wait 'ere until we know it is the farmer,'
whispered Pierre. 'Something is not right,' he
added.

In the distance we saw the dim headlights of
not just one vehicle but several. Pierre had a
bad feeling about it. 'Please, quiet! do not make
a noise. We must move further back from these
trees and lie down,' he said.

We reached the bushes just in time before a
convoy of three Nazi tanks came into view. The
tanks started slowing down and stopped just

where we had been sitting. The Germans were laughing and shouting and climbing out of the tanks. Three soldiers waded into the bushes for a pee. Sid was trying to keep me from barking by feeding me treats to calm me down.

More soldiers had climbed down and started wandering about the field. They were heading straight for our hideout in the bushes. Pierre knew we would be captured if we were found. Keeping still was my biggest problem as I was straining on my leash to go and see their Nazi visitors.

Sweat dripped down Sid's forehead, as it always did when he felt threatened. One of the soldiers then spotted boot prints in the mud and called his mates over to look. Together they slowly started tracking the prints straight towards our hideout. 'It could all be over soon,' whispered Sid rubbing his eyes.

At that moment a big cloud drifted over the moon and the whole field went dark. Someone was shouting from the road and the tanks' engines started up again. The four soldiers turned and marched back towards the road.

'Phew! that was close,' said Sid mopping his brow with his sleeve. But Pierre was very worried.

'Our friend will pass them on the road and will be stopped and questioned. But, 'e is a Resistance fighter so I hope he weel know what to do. We weel wait 'ere for him to come.'

The moon was high in the sky and more clouds were building up blocking out its light and then it got very dark as there were no lights for miles around.

We sat for some time, listening to the sounds of the night. I was excited to hear the foxes and the frogs. Very close by, an owl hooted - three times, and each time it was closer than the last.

'Ahh! Sssh.... listen,' whispered Pierre. 'Did you hear the Owl?' Then it hooted another three times. 'I theenk it is 'im - Gabriel - Ah oui! it is 'im! That is his call. Perhaps he decided not to use the road.'

Suddenly, something, or someone was pushing through the bushes behind us. My hackles were up. I leapt forward and growled.

'Pierre, Pierre, C'est moi, Gabriel,' said a deep gruff voice as a tall stout man wearing wellington boots and a knitted hat came trundling out of the bushes waving a big stick.

'This is my cousin,' explained Pierre. Gabriel shook hands with Sid, squeezing his little hand so tightly Sid winced. 'Suivez moi!' whispered Gabriel. And so, we all trudged across three fields to a big, dimly lit, rambling farmhouse where a hot meal of chicken stew was bubbling cooked by Chloe, Gabriel's wife. I was given meat and gravy in a dish which was delicious!

After our meal, Pierre translated what Gabriel's plan was. 'We will leave at sunrise tomorrow and go in the farm lorry towards Paris. I will drop you near Amiens. Someone else will take you into Paris. We cannot use the main roads as already the Germans are heading for Paris. But, I know other routes we can use - and hide if we need to. You must have your papers ready in case we get stopped and say you are going to the British Embassy in Paris and then back to England,' explained Pierre.
'Well that is true, except I have to find my family first,' said Sid hopefully.

It was a long journey the next day which should only have taken two hours, but on the back roads and through villages it took six hours. There were lots of people leaving Paris to escape the Nazis. 'I just pray we can reach and save my daughter, her husband and my granddaughter in time!' said Sid with teary eyes.

CHAPTER FIVE

HOLOCAUST TRAIN

Prisoners on Holocaust train

The following night we said goodbye to our good friends Pierre and Gabriel. At 11.30pm a small Citroen van chugged into the yard driven by Marcel, another Resistance activist. He was on his way back to Paris and had agreed to take us. It was 145 kms on a direct route, but our journey would take twice as long. We had to use back roads as already German checkpoints were being set up.

'I 'ave heard people are trying to leave Amiens

for Dunkirk as the Germans are already on their way to Amiens,' said Marcel. But all Sid knew was he had to carry on to Paris to find his family. It was a race against time.

Marcel had grown up in Paris so knew it very well indeed. Four hours later we had reached the outskirts and were on our way to the British Embassy when suddenly, I sensed great danger so howled loudly. Sid knew something was up, and told Marcel to stop. 'Buddy only does this for a reason,' explained Sid. So, although Marcel was not pleased, he pulled over into a side street.

Sid undid my lead and followed me. I stood rigid, ears pricked and hackles up looking down the hill in front of us. Then, Sid and Marcel saw it: a huge flag with a swastika being carried by a troop of German soldiers on horses waving a banner which read "Juden Raus!" (Jews out!) which they kept chanting. They were only about 200 metres away.

'Quickly, we must go another way!' shouted Marcel who gave me a big thank you hug and a treat for alerting them. 'I 'ope your Embassy is still open,' said Marcel in a worried voice.

We had to take a long diversion via the railway station. But something was wrong. We saw people being loaded into cattle wagon trains by German soldiers. I became very agitated, so Sid knew he had to check.

'My daughter might be there!' said Sid desperately, but Marcel refused to go any further. 'We will get arrested too! probably shot. I cannot go, but I will wait here for you.'

Sid and I mingled with the onlookers behind a barricade and watched the terrible scene of thousands of men being loaded into the trains. Some were hanging out of the top of the cattle wagons and crying out in distress.

'Come Buddy, we must go and check Ruth's apartment.' He turned to go back to Marcel's car, but I would not move - for a good reason. Instead I whined and tried to get to the front of the crowd. I sniffed the air and the ground, and picked up a familiar scent above all the others. People were shouting and protesting as there were five more wagons filled with women and children. A man told Sid that some women and children were arrested trying to leave Paris and that a major deportation of women would happen in 1942.

Then, something extraordinary happened. Above all the confusion, Sid thought he heard a woman's voice singing. It sounded familiar but full of anguish. It was the sound of a lullaby. Not just any lullaby, but one only known to his daughter Ruth which her mother used to sing to her. 'Is she singing it to comfort Meira?' said Sid. He looked desperate. 'I am sure it must be Ruth with Meira on the train,' he cried and watched with an aching heart as the train slowly chugged out of the station.

It was time to do something - and fast! so I began sniffing the ground using my strongest senses for tracking until I found Ruth's scent.

'That's it!' shouted Sid. He pulled me back to Marcel. 'We need to follow the train now! My dog will track it. He has picked up Ruth's scent.'

Quickly, Marcel left a message with a friend at a cafe to follow us with a bicycle in his van as we knew the train was heading for Poland - and Auschwitz.

We followed the train for some miles as it was going slowly. But then the road changed direction. There was just enough time for Sid to unload the bicycle from the van. And so, we began to follow the railway line through the woods. It was difficult though as there were no pathways through the thick forest. All the way I managed to keep pace - tracking. But a big problem worried Sid - how could he rescue Ruth and Meira?

CHAPTER SIX

THE HOLE

Inside the dark, hot, smelly, overcrowded train, women comforted each other. Some were crying and wailing. Others chanted prayers. It seemed all hope was gone - as there was no escape from the cattle wagon trains.

The only other hole in the carriage, apart from the small air vents at the top, was in the corner of the wagon. It was less than 40 cms across used for drainage after cleaning the carriage. But it was being used as a latrine so had a foul smell and was caked with human and animal excrement.

Ruth held Meira in her arms. 'We must be brave and try to get off this train my little one,' she told her daughter trying to sound hopeful. 'There is a chance we can climb down through that hole when the train stops,' she explained. Meira nodded. 'Yes mama. I will do it if you do it,' she said eager to escape the terrible wagon.

Ruth held her nose as she examined the disgusting hole. Looking down she could see the railway track. Being small and slim Ruth reckoned she was just big enough to squeeze through it, or was she? If she got stuck, she might break her back and legs and would surely die. Meira would certainly get through.

There was no choice. It was a risk they had to take, but first the train had to slow right down - perhaps to load more coal. The other women in the wagon were too afraid but agreed to help her and little Meira in any way they could. Ruth never knew that outside, Sid and I were trying to keep up with the train

Another hour or so passed before the train started slowing down. The sun dipped behind distant hills and inside the cattle wagon it was almost pitch black. Ruth felt sick as she stood over the stinking latrine. She would go first, then the women would have to guide little Meira down. Just the thought of freedom kept Ruth brave and spurred her on. She fastened her hat with a scarf and tied a long cloth, torn from her dress, over Meira's nose and mouth.

The brakes made a long, loud screech as the train juddered to a halt. The women in the carriage urged her on. 'Go, go now quickly!'

Some kissed her farewell as they helped her
to the hole. But even though she was slim,
it was not possible to get through. Then one
big woman took off her boot and used it as a
hammer to loosen the grunge on the sides of the
hole. It gave Ruth another 10 cms - just enough
to slowly and painfully push through the stench
of the opening and onto the railway track.
Meira was quickly lowered after her.

They both lay stretched out. Meira was
vomiting and crying softly as was Ruth. But
they had to lie very, very still as there were
guards on patrol stretching their legs, as well
as surveillance by searchlights along the train
convoy.

The guards were smoking and laughing and -
getting closer. Ruth could see their big boots
- kicking stones about. She could even see
them dropping cigarette buts close by them.
If the guards bent down they would spot Ruth
and Meira at once. Then one soldier jumped
down the bank for a pee. His head was level
with the track as he came back. 'Be still!' Ruth
whispered to Meira. Ruth closed her eyes
fearing it was all over, all in vain, as she slipped
into unconsciousness.

The intense juddering of the train and hiss of the steam engine slowly woke Ruth. 'Mama, mama! wake up, please mama,' cried Meira in a panic. Then Ruth remembered the horror of their escape through the hole. But, they were still on the track and alive. The soldier had not seen them. The under carriage of the train was skimming over them only about 20 cms above their heads. It rumbled and hooted then slowed to a stop again. 'Oh NO, no! they must have discovered we're missing,' Ruth feared.

But there was another reason. A stray goat had wandered onto the railway line and trapped its leg in the sleepers. A soldier jumped down, released the animal then kicked it over the bank. 'Ha! Sie sind ein Köder dumm gooat?' (Are you a decoy stupid goat?) he shouted. Nervously he looked round to see if anyone was in the trees, waving his rifle in front of him aggressively. 'Achtung! Was geht hier vor?' (Who goes there?) he shouted out. But only the wind rustled the leaves. It was too dark to see, so he backed up still looking around him until he reached the train, then climbed up quickly, rifle still cocked. The train rolled on noisily, gathering speed.

Ruth and Meira didn't dare move until it had disappeared.

They lay trembling. Meira was cold and feeling very sick indeed. Slowly Ruth pulled herself up. Her legs and arms were weak and bleeding, her clothes torn and her curly brown hair matted with dirt and grunge from the latrine.

Little Meira looked a bit better: her plaited hair still neat and quite clean. Ruth took her in her arms and started to laugh, softly at first and then hysterically with tears rolling down her face. She felt drunk with fatigue. 'Sssh! mama, we must be quiet!' 'Yes, and now we must run my darling, quickly!' They rolled down the bank just like the goat had done, over and over into stinging nettles and brambles. They hurt but Ruth relished their herby aromas. At the bottom there was a small stream where Ruth washed them both.

CHAPTER SEVEN

DOGS

'We must keep moving and keep warm my darling!' she told Meira. The woods were dark and scary - full of shadows and strange noises. But soon Ruth's eyes became accustomed to the blackness and her vision cleared.

'We'll be owls and see through the dark,' she told Meira. Amazingly, it worked and guided by the stars they started to walk westwards - away from the route of the train and its deadly destination. After two hours Meira could go no further. 'Mama, I cannot walk anymore. Please, can we stop now?' she pleaded, crying with exhaustion. So, like two forest creatures, they gathered twigs, fallen branches and leaves to make a bed. Sleep came quickly while all around were the sounds of frogs squawking, crickets chirping and somewhere an owl hooted.

The warm, early morning sun glinted through the forest canopy and spread softly over the earth, caressing Ruth's bruised face. She stretched slowly, aching all over, but happy to be alive. But just then, she heard another sound and shivered with fear.'Dogs, I can hear dogs! They are after us,' she said to herself.

'Meira, wake up, we have to hurry now. We must run as fast as we can!' But Meira was slow to stand up. They had not eaten for nearly two days and her legs were numb and lifeless.

'My legs mama. They will not move. I cannot go on.' And she started to sob and hold on to Ruth. 'All right my little one, we will stay here. Maybe they will be kind to us. Let's lie down behind this tree and cover our faces,' whispered Ruth, hugging Meira and trying to sound calm. 'Just close your eyes. Mama is here and no harm will come to you.' Ruth prayed as she had never prayed before.

But, it was all over, boots were crunching through the leaves and Ruth could hear the barking of a savage dog getting closer and closer. Instinctively, she held her hands over her daughter's head and ears for protection and closed her own eyes.

The dog reached their tree, salivating and panting, ready for attack. Then, It pressed its big wet nose on her head and then on Meira's exposed neck and began to - lick! and lick! and whine and lick again! Meira buried her head into Ruth's breast while Ruth lay motionless, eyes closed, afraid to look up.

Suddenly, a gloved hand was stroking the hair away from her face. Silence followed. The dog was pulled away and sat huffing and puffing. After a while she heard a voice, not talking, but gently humming a tune. It was a lullaby - one that only she, her mama and her Pa, Sid knew.

Ruth wondered whether she was dreaming. Slowly she moved one hand upwards. It was held gently and stroked in a comforting way. Even the dog put his paw on Ruth's hand.

'Ruth, Ruth, it's me, Pa,' he whispered. 'Buddy has been tracking the train ever since it left Paris. He's a miracle dog and he's saved you both my little ones.'

Painfully Ruth lifted her head and focussed on her father's unshaven face through teary eyes. 'Meira, look, grandpa and Buddy have come to rescue us!' After many hugs and kisses Ruth told their tale of escape and of those hundreds of others left on the death train. She had no idea where Abe, her husband was, as he was forcibly taken long before.

'Others might have tried your method of escape too,' said Sid. 'If so, and they are on the run, then the Nazis will surely try and recapture them and they will use dogs, so now we must get to a safe place fast.'

Sid's bicycle was large and had a back seat which Meira and Ruth were just able to balance on, but it wasn't easy and progress was slow through the woods as we could not risk the roads through to Abbeville.

When Sid left Paris, his friend, Gabriel had given him names of cafes and farms where we could find shelter in Piccardie as the German forces were pushing hard to reach Paris.

Then, one dreadful night the Germans reached the farm where we were sleeping in a barn. I smelt them coming and warned Sid and Ruth long before so that we were able to hide high in the rafters. The soldiers kicked the door open and marched in. But staring at them ready to charge were two massive stud bulls. The men were just able to shut the barn door in time and run for it!

CHAPTER EIGHT

'INVISIBLE'

Eventually, we reached Saint-Valery-sur-Somme
where a small fishing boat named 'Invisible'
was waiting. I was the main lookout on deck
for soldiers and twice more I saved us from
being discovered. But it meant Sid, Ruth - and
Meira too - had to dive underneath the boat
for ten minutes only using their snorkels as an
emergency. The random checks were getting
more frequent, so our escape had to be at night
when the soldiers were enjoying the French wine
and food in local cafes.

Everything was ready on board 'Invisible'. The
skipper called himself Napoleon. He was short
and stout, with a round, red weatherbeaten face.
He liked to laugh a lot and sing songs. Over
his balding head he wore a knitted cap pulled
down over his ears and in one ear he wore a
gold earring. Mainly, he enjoyed a dangerous
challenge, especially taking on the Germans!
'They will not catch Napoleon's boat. It is
invisible!' he laughed showing his big white
teeth.

Sid had sailed on fishing boats many times so was a useful deck hand. I enjoyed it too as I wore a dog's life jacket and stood at the bow. Sid explained to Napoleon how I would warn them of any trouble. They didn't have long to wait. I jumped down growling. My hackles were up. I had heard the stomp of soldiers' boots at the far end of the harbour long before they came into view

Ruth and Meira quickly went down into the cabin where there was a deep bunk - a bit like a coffin - hidden under another bunk and more planking and oars where the life vests were kept. It was not very safe so they had to be extra quiet.

'Quickly, we must go NOW!' said Napoleon sensing the Nazis were very close. Sid cast off and jumped back into the boat. The speed limit in the harbour was just 5 knots so it was a very slow journey to the harbour exit. Clouds were building in the west and the wind was strengthening. 'It is blowing well for us. We make good speed!' said Napoleon humming a song Sid didn't recognise.

Then, Sid noticed they had company. Another

small boat to the stern and two others, one
each side of 'Invisible' were gathering speed.
'Ah! now we 'ave some fun, yes Sid?' beamed
Napoleon. But Sid looked very scared. 'What's
going on? I don't understand. They are German
patrol boats!' 'Ah, yes, I think so,' chuckled
Napoleon hissing through his teeth.
Sid felt his world slipping away. What had he
done trusting this man? He sat on the deck with
his head in his hands. I quickly jumped onto
the deck too trying to console him. 'Invisible'
slowed right down while the patrol boats came
along side. When he looked up, he saw a lot of
Germans sniggering and boxes being thrown
over to Napoleon to catch. Then the skipper
of the patrol boat shouted. "Il est sûr. Bon
voyage!" (It is safe. Have a good trip)

'Invisible' gathered speed and was soon out
of the harbour and into the open sea heading
across the Channel for England - and home!
Napoleon was whistling and singing, then
laughing. 'I told you my friend, not to worry.
We are all actors on a stage. They were friends
of mine dressed like the enemy. Clever, yes?'
and he laughed some more.

Ruth and Sid were always grateful to their

French Resistance friends - and saviours,
as millions did not escape. But Ruth was
heartbroken that Abe was not with them sailing
to freedom. Meira asked about him constantly.

When, eventually they arrived home in London,
Sid wrote a letter to the Prime Minister
thanking him for his help and telling him of
their great escape from the Nazis. Ruth and
Meira were able to describe the conditions
inside the cattle wagons and of the thousands
who didn't escape. Officials from MI5 and MI6
visited Sid and Ruth and took statements of
their experiences for future evidence of Nazi
War crimes.

Once again, I too was honoured as an
'extraordinary dog' and recorded as a War hero
for my work. And, as a special 'thank you'
I was introduced to Sheeba, a very beautiful
glossy black Lab with kind brown eyes - which
she passed on to most of our puppies and future
generations. It was the best present ever for me!

Three turbulent years of War passed with
terrible losses on both sides and atrocities in
the concentration camps where millions of
jews and others were murdered. Families were

ripped apart, never to see their loved ones ever again.

Meanwhile, Sid and I went on to rescue hundreds of people from the bombed streets of London. Then, one day in March 1944 Sid received a telegram from the War Office. It told him to take me to the War Dog Training School to train for active duty in France.

Most people volunteered their dogs for service but because of my so-called extraordinary reputation, I had been specially recommended by the Prime Minister himself! What happened to me is told in the next story 'Called up'.

CHAPTER NINE

AFTER THE WAR

Time to "Dig for Victory"

Ruth was 36 and Meira was nine years old when the War in Europe officially ended in May 1945. Life became quiet again, but every commodity was in short supply and the government enforced rationing of food and other goods. People were encouraged to "Dig for Victory" by the government to supplement their diets.

Sid was blessed with a house and a garden in London left to him by his wife when she died in 1933 of rheumatic fever. The garden was to provide Sid, his daughter Ruth and granddaughter Meira with a good source of food during and after the War years. Ruth and Meira became good gardeners.

It was while Ruth was digging one warm summer's day in June,1945 when I was stretched out under the apple tree when, quite suddenly, I picked up a familiar scent so jumped up and scampered off. Ten minutes or so later, Ruth heard the garden gate creak open. 'I could really do with a cup of tea Pa,' she shouted, not looking up.

Ruth was still kneeling in the potato patch when there was a scuffling sound behind her. 'Now what? you crazy dog!' she muttered. But as she turned her head she found she was looking at a pair of ragged and strange army boots. One was laced up with a yellow lace! She fell backwards in surprise and gasped.

Looking down at her was the face of a much thinner, but smiling - Abe! Their celebrations never, ever ended and they lived each day as if it were their last - in contentment and with immense gratitude for their amazing survival.**"**

JUMPING FROM TRAINS

After the War, many heroic stories came to light of desperate Jews jumping from the moving cattle wagons to escape the death camps, such as the two men who prised open the bars on a small window using smuggled tools. A report read: *"Perched on the outside edge of the cattle wagon they clung on desperately trying to avoid the searchlight guards cast over the rail convoy. When the train went into a corner, they used the concave shadow to jump. An estimated 764 people managed to escape the Holocaust by jumping to freedom from the Nazi trains carrying them to the death camps from France,*

Holland and Belgium."

(Next - 'CALLED UP')

CALLED UP

CHAPTER ONE

THE TELEGRAM

"After a scary dream I woke up with a shiver and noticed how slowly my tail wagged - as it usually did when I felt unsure about things. In fact, I'm convinced my crazy tail has got a brain of its own! My knees wobbled and ached a bit as I stood up - a sign of cold weather I reminded myself.

A loud knock on the front door brought Sid thumping down the stairs so I ran out too. Sid's face went white when he saw it was a telegram messenger boy.

'A telegram for Sid Malkovich from the War Office,' he chirped. It was March 1944.

Through the open door I sniffed the bleak, frosty morning air and was about to race around the garden like I normally did until I saw how worried Sid was.

He slowly read the telegram.

"Please bring your dog to the War Dog Training School at Potters Bar, Hertfordshire at 09.00 hrs on Monday, 13th March. Make sure your dog has a valid Vet's Health Certificate."

I woofed softly and looked up at Sid who was blowing his nose and wiping his eyes. 'That's just two days away!' he said in a shaky voice. I whined and put my paw on Sid's leg to comfort him.

'Well then, tomorrow we'll have fun with Ruth and Meira before you go,' he said more cheerfully. But I knew that inside Sid felt sad and totally shocked as he loved me very much.

'Gosh boy, we've been together since 1939 at the start of this terrible War. We've survived the worst of the London Blitz and saved hundreds of people - all because of your extraordinary instincts,' said Sid proudly stroking my head.

'You even helped to rescue my lovely daughter, Ruth, and grand daughter Meira from the Nazis in 1941. How special is that?' he recalled with full admiration for me - his four legged friend.

'And to think we are now living here with them

in London. Well, I have to pinch myself most days to believe it!'

But the War was getting worse and the army were looking for suitable dogs to train for War combat duties such as - messengers, mine detectors, search and rescue, sniffing out the enemy and even para-dogs to parachute behind enemy lines.

Advertisements appeared in local papers for people to lend their dogs to be trained and taken for War duties. Out of many thousands of unsuitable dogs, six thousand were eventually recruited.

But news of my so-called talents had spread straight from the highest source - the Prime Minister's office, Winston Churchill, who had first met Sid and me in1940 when we tracked down two German spies in the heart of London.

Well, Sid knew he couldn't refuse such an important mission for King and country, so had to face letting me go, even though it meant I would be taken to the front-line, perhaps never to return.

Sid checked his watch - 08.00 hrs. He kissed his daughter Ruth and little Meira goodbye and fixed my lead.

'Oh Buddy! we shall miss you every day!' sobbed Meira as she hugged my big neck with her tiny hands. 'Yes - so please come home safe and sound,' added Ruth as she kissed my head.

'Come on boy, let's go and see what they want with you. Whatever happens, we'll stick together!' said Sid - but without much conviction! his voice breaking up a bit.

Tall iron gates enclosed a sentry box with two metre high wire fencing stretching out each side of the field. 'Looks like a prisoner of War camp!' he said sadly. Inside the box sat a portly army sergeant with a bulging red face, round spectacles and a grumpy look.

'I.D. and fill out this form,' he said abruptly without a smile. 'Rude swine!' Sid thought. 'Is this really necessary - taking my dog?' asked Sid hoping for a last minute reprieve. The sergeant scowled angrily. 'Just do it mate - unless you want the mutt put down,' he hissed. Sid raged inside and felt like punching the officer's red nose. But he knew that would only make matters worse and I might suffer if he did.

With a heavy heart Sid filled out the form. The sergeant snatched it back and examined it carefully.

'Oooo! the Dickin Medal eh? Now isn't he a clever mutt!' sneered the officer. 'Time to prove what you're really made of at this school,' he added maliciously.

Sid winced and made a fist to control his angst.

'Err, I'd like to see him every day,' said Sid sternly.

'Ha! forget that!' shouted the officer.'The dog will be army property from now on, like any other soldier serving King and country. But you can have him back after the War's over - if he survives!' Sid was just too sad and gutted to reply. The officer looked at Sid's face and felt a bit sorry for him. 'The fact is mate this War won't last long - since we've got the Jerries on the run!'

Sid bent down and gave me a big hug. 'Do the best you can old friend and - I'll be seeing you.' I whined and gave Sid lots of gentle kisses to wash his tears away.

The iron gate creaked open and out marched a

tall, muscly man with tattoos up his arm. His name was Fred. 'Do you want to take off his lead or shall I?' he asked. Slowly Sid unbuckled my collar and petted my nose. Fred quickly replaced it with a fat leather lead and collar.

Despite his rough appearance, Fred had a kindly voice and sparkling eyes. But all along I knew what was happening. I barked and whined as loud as I could at leaving my best friend.

'It's like taking the children to school for the first time' muttered Sid, tears of regret stinging his pale cheeks. 'I should have gone far away and taken Buddy with me. Gone into hiding!' The possibility he might never see me again was just too much to bear, so he pushed the thought to the back of his mind.

Eleven other dogs were in the compound tied up outside their kennels. They jumped up and whined when they saw me. Some barked and strained on their leashes. Others snarled loudly - all except one, a border collie who reminded me of my lovely friend Peg who died in the Blitz. I immediately wanted to meet her.

The gates clanged shut which made me jump.
Sid held the wire fence and watched me being
led across the compound towards the other
dogs. I stopped, turned, looked back at Sid and
held up my paw in a last farewell to my true
friend. I pulled hard on my lead and tried to run
back to Sid, but Fred wrenched me to heel with
such force it made me choke for air, whining
like a puppy.

'No going back now boy. You're 'ere forever!
so get used to it!' he commanded.
The officer in the sentry box was watching.
'You'd better go now mate. You'll upset the
animal and yourself more if he sees you.'

'Yes, for his sake I'll go now,' mumbled Sid as
he turned slowly and walked back to the van,
his head downcast in utter misery.

Fred paraded me in front of the other dogs
so they could sniff me out. 'Grrrrrrr - woof!"
growled one big German Shepherd who didn't
want me too close.
When we reached the border collie, I stopped
and walked slowly towards her. But Fred
yanked me away quickly.
'Watch it! she's a vicious one. She'll bite your

throat will Spam - silent and sneaky she is.
She's had me spam fritters off me plate a few
times. That's how she got her name - "Spam".

I laughed inside, wagging my tail. 'yum, yum
to spam!- whatever that is!' I thought licking
my lips. Spam sat up straight looking at me
with her big soft brown eyes.

'Closer, come closer!' she woofed gently,
fluttering her long black eyelashes. So, I sidled
up to her. Slowly, she sniffed me all over. Then
suddenly, she leapt backwards. 'You're already a
Blitz dog!' she snarled. I leapt back too and shook
myself. I wondered how she knew 'So, what if I
am?' I woofed proudly.
'It means that you've already got War experience
- so why are you in this training school sharing
our food? If my dinner is smaller today, then
you'll have to share yours with me!' she barked
wagging her tail. 'Is she joking or not?' I
thought. But I'm always confused by female
dogs. What's more, my kennel was quite close to
Spam's. I scratched my ear to think about it.

Just then, the CLANG CLANG of someone
banging on a tin started all the dogs barking. It
meant dinnertime!

'WOW and YUM!' I thought as a big bowl of real meat mixed with greens, biscuits and gravy was plonked down in front of me. I was very hungry so got stuck in straight away. 'Better eat fast before Spam comes over' I thought. Later I found out how lucky I was, as dogs in the training school were fed good food to keep them healthy for their War duties. It made me feel sorry for the dogs on the outside though - starving because of the War.

That night I cried a lot as I missed my rug by the fire sitting with Sid, the games in the garden with Meira and the special treats from Ruth - which were our secret! I whined and whimpered for a long time. 'I guess this is homesickness,' I thought. But I knew it wouldn't be long before I saw them again. It was my last happy hope before I fell fast asleep.

CHAPTER TWO

TRAINING BEGINS

Detecting mines in France

Ding-a-ling-a-ling! rang the wake up bell. I stretched and shook myself, then guzzled lots of water and burped. A bright dawn was breaking and the birds were twittering in the fresh March air. Most dogs were awake including Spam who was staring at me in a very bleary eyed way.

The first exercise was a test to sort which of us dogs would be right for combat. Not even Spam knew what was going to happen. And it had to be done before breakfast. Later we realised why.

The gate into the compound creaked open and out marched a brigade of twelve big WOMEN! in uniform. Of course I barked my approval and hoped they might be like Ruth who gave me sneaky treats! Then all the dogs barked and wouldn't stop.

'SILENCE!' shouted the female sergeant. 'We are from the Auxiliary Territorial Service (ATS) and your kennel-maids, here to test you for battle!' she added sternly. 'Go to it girls. Pick your canine!'

One by one the girls picked a dog. A very big girl stood in front of me. I looked up defiantly. 'I could pull her down - no problem,' I thought with mischievous intentions! But "Big Pam" as she was known was a very strong lady indeed and was used to big dogs. 'So Buddy, let's see what you are made of. I shall be watching you!'

'Leash up and walk on!' shouted the sergeant.
The kennel-maids walked us around the
compound for about ten minutes to settle us
down. But my hackles were up as I knew
something was about to happen.

Out shuffled the head trainer carrying a big box.
He reached inside and took out some objects
which he started to throw about. Suddenly -
SWISH, BANG, BOOM! They were 'thunder
flashes' to test which dogs could cope under
gunfire. The dogs which showed signs of stress
were rejected and returned to their owners. But
some owners didn't want their dogs back, so
they were taken away and put down.

'If I'd have known that I would have pretended
to be stressed so that I could have gone home to
Sid!' I realised.
But I was a Blitz dog so gunfire and explosions
didn't faze me and I wasn't going to give in
and be a wimp!

'Stress over here!' shouted a kennel-maid. 'And
here!' shouted another. Six dogs had to be taken
away. Three were trying to be sick but had no
breakfast to bring up.
Anxiously I looked around for Spam. She sat

by her kennel maid shaking a bit - but had survived the test.'What will they do to us next?' I wondered.

The next day, the remaining six of us had a rest - just walks, food and socialising! 'Ypeee! we're free for today!' I barked spinning in circles. 'Ohhh! no, no, no! I don't feel free,' moaned Spam. 'Can't run about in the long grass or chase sheep, can I?' Poor Spam. I stretched out my paw and patted her back. 'You will again - but not today, so let's enjoy what we can right now! then tomorrow won't seem so bad,' I woofed.

A big truck chugged noisily into the compound next morning. Black smoke belched from its giant exhaust pipe."AAAA-chooo! AAAA-chooo!" sneezed the dogs one after the other. 'C'mon you lot - jump on board!' shouted Matt one of the trainers.

It was a bumpy ride. 'Ouchee! my head!' whined Spam as she was flung to the side of the truck. The other dogs were not happy either and lay flat to keep from toppling over. A sudden s c r e e c h of brakes stopped the truck - dead! throwing us about in the back like loose footballs.

'Ahhhh! my ears! what's that loud noise?'
yelped Spam. The back doors were opened
and we quickly leapt down from the truck to
investigate. We were on a runway where four
enormous transport planes ROARED! all
around us.

'Great! perhaps we're going on a journey
somewhere nice and far away' I thought. But
no! we just had to sit for hours inside the planes
whilst their propellers kept spinning. Our
handler shouted: 'This is to get you dogs used
to the noises of war. If you can't hack it, then
you're no good to us!'

All the dogs put up with it, but Spam was on
edge all the time. 'Another day of this and
I'll make a run for it!' she whined. 'Don't
be a woos!' I barked. 'You can't just give in.
Tomorrow will be better. You'll see.'

I was right. First, our lady kennel maids
returned. 'Some interesting sniffing exercises
today on how to detect explosives and
gunpowder,' shouted the sergeant. We all found
it easy- including Spam. After all, a dog's sense
of smell is mind-blowing - being 1,000 to 10
million times more powerful than a human's

as, depending on the breed, dogs use between 125 million to 300 million scent glands! But a human only has about 5 million.

Our training got more intense with mock battles including gunfire, explosions and marauding tanks. We were taught how to track down the enemy, carry messages and even deliver telephone lines strapped to our backs. So we had to be fearless, fast and aware of how to duck and run while being fired at. And even what to do if our masters were captured or killed. The specialised training lasted for over two months.

CHAPTER THREE

THE 'FEARLESS FOUR'

Parachuting dogs behind enemy lines

Four dogs in the squad were chosen for even

more dangerous work - for parachuting -
yes parachuting! behind enemy lines. Their
job was to sniff out landmines, to warn of
the approaching enemy and to deliver vital
messages. Eventually, Alfie the German
shepherd, Tigger the chocolate Labrador, Spam
the border collie, and I the black Labrador were
chosen. We were nicknamed 'The Fearless
Four'.

'We are the 'paradogs' and shall fly through the
air!' woofed Tigger who was always up for an
exciting jump in the air! Everyone loved Tigger
as he made people laugh, no matter how bad
a day it was. And Alfie was a good creeping
stalker. He sussed things about people and
situations that no one else could see - but took
his time about it.

On the morning of our first test flight, we didn't
feel "fearless" - just agitated - and hungry!
'Strictly no breakfast for you four until after
your jumps. Something to look forward to eh?'
said Fred with a happy smile and some doggie
pats on the head to calm us down. 'But, after
you've jumped - then you'll each get a special
treat!' We all smacked our lips and wondered
what that treat would be. I woofed in approval

while Tigger reared up in his begging pose looking hopeful.

Fred was one of the paratroopers assigned to jump with a dog along with Jim, Harry and Dan. 'Oooh! I'm pleased I'm with Fred!' woofed Spam. 'He's cool!' But Alfie was still wary of Jim. 'Don't know whether to like him yet!' he groused. Tigger bounced up and landed PLONK on his two back legs 'Wheee! Harry for hairy Tigger - that's me!' I was excited too. My tail wagged very fast! 'Hooray! I'm with daring Dan - our leader!'

There were other paratroopers on the same flight that morning who lined up to jump first. Us dogs were next. Spam was shaking a bit and was pleased to be the last out as she watched the technique of the others.

Dan and I went first. We crouched, hovering over the open hatch. The icy cold air gushed into the aircraft. I gulped as I sniffed millions of smells wafting up from the void. 'Off you go boy. Enjoy your flight. I'm right behind you,' shouted Dan as he gently eased me out of the aircraft. My parachute soon sprang open and then I was floating and flying like a bird on the wind.

When Dan jumped he called out to me. He was about 30 metres away. But suddenly a strong gust of wind blew me sideways and made me wobble. I felt cold and scared. 'Stay calm boy. I'm close by you Buddy,' he shouted. Then all was well again and I wagged my tail to thank Dan.

Minute by minute the ground zoomed closer - and closer - and closer! - until THUD! Well, sort of! as my parachute pulled me along for a bit. Then I remembered what Dan had said so just rolled over and over in the soft grass. Dan was rolling over too.

I shook myself and barked loudly for Dan. He dashed over and gave me a big hug - and my special treat - a big hunk of juicy meat. 'Well done boy! What a team we'll make eh?'

The other dogs landed safely too and were gobbling up their treats with gusto. So that was the routine - jump, land and eat. Very soon we really were "The Fearless Four" and became expert paradogs leaping out of aircraft without any coaxing - thinking of our treats on landing!

Finally, at the end of May 1944 we were

declared "trained and ready for battle". The timing was just right and our help became crucial in what was to become a vital war combat against the Nazis - the D-Day landings.

People, hopeful that the War would end after D-Day on June 6th 1944, were sad and frightened that it still continued and that the Germans had made new and even more deadly weapons.

It was discovered that German scientists had been secretly designing deadly rocket missiles which could be launched from France and Belgium to travel across the Channel to London. These were known as V-1 and V-2 rockets - Hitler's lethal 'vengeance weapons'. These flying bombs were nicknamed 'doodlebugs' or 'buzz bombs' because they made a horrible droning noise. When the noise stopped, people knew they had just 15 seconds to escape the huge blast that followed. 'Listen out for doodlebugs and lie flat to escape the blast,' people were told. But either they didn't remember or have time to respond and thousands were killed.

It was a cold, moonless night when we, The Fearless Four, were rounded up with other paradogs to make our first real sortie across the Channel to help the troops. It was only the German shepherd Alfie and I who sussed it wasn't just an ordinary exercise. Our handlers were very quiet and tense. I saw Jim, Alfie's handler, wiping his eyes after looking at his mum's photograph and saying something softly. Jim was the youngest handler and it was his first sortie too. Tigger was just being Tigger. PLONK! BANG! he threw a ball at Spam then chased her to get it back, snarling playfully. Dan stood up straight in front of us. He had a serious look on his face. 'Now - listen up! Tonight when we land you will be tracking the real enemy using your amazing senses. You will be our ears and our eyes on the beaches and in the dark forests. As in training, proceed with stealth and silence at all times. We will be watching and relying on your signals. We'll keep together as a troop, so stay as close as you can - but only if you can. We're heading for the front line.'

Faces dropped. No one spoke. Alfie looked up at Jim his master as he felt him shiver. He rested his paw on Jim's boot. I watched in silent admiration as Jim stroked Alfie's strong, proud head and for the first time noticed a deep bond between them. 'Friends forever! Thank you Alfie,' said Jim quietly. From that moment on, I knew that he and Alfie would be strong friends - no matter what.

CHAPTER FOUR

LAND AHOY!

Out on the dark runway, the wind blew cold
and hard as we all boarded the C-47 Skytrain
bound for France to be dropped behind enemy
lines. Alfie and I were together in one plane and
Spam and Tigger in another. Constant checks
were made of our harnesses and parachutes
during the journey. Everything seemed spot on.
For Alfie and me it was just another exercise.
The droning sound of the engines made me
feel sleepy so I enjoyed a snooze and dreamt of
meaty treats on landing!

Before the French coast came into view, Dan,
Jim and the other paratroopers did warm
up exercises in the aircraft. 'Right boys -
quadriceps, hamstrings, spinal stretches,
forward bends, then twenty push-ups,'
suggested Dan who went first. 'We have to be
on top form for what lies ahead.'

'Land ahoy!' announced the pilot cheerfully.
He knew the hard part was coming up - the
jump - especially for us dogs. 'OK we'll go
first,' said Dan bravely. The hatch was opened

and as usual the blast of windrush hit us first.
'Now - go boy, go!' shouted Dan easing me out
of the hatch. Dan followed and gasped from the
buffeting of the aircraft's slipstream.
I drifted down with my legs outstretched which
made me look very peculiar. Dan laughed and
whistled out to me. My tail wagged vigorously
in response. Alfie and Jim jumped safely too,
floating through the silence of the fresh, earthy
night air which was cool and comforting after
the stuffy aircraft. We all ran for cover through
the long grass and into the bushes.

But Dan was troubled.'I haven't seen Fred,
Spam, Harry or Tigger come down yet. Hope
they're okay,' he thought. Then suddenly, RAT-
a-TAT, TAT, TAT - the dreaded stuttering sound
of rifle fire broke the silence and yellow flashes
from anti aircraft missiles blazed deadly trails
through the clouds. 'Damn it!' cursed Dan
'They must have jumped late so they're now
off course!'

While the sky burned, the four of us watched
in horror as many other paratroopers and their
dogs were shot down before landing. 'Oh
STOP! STOP!' cried Jim.

'Those evil Nazis!! We'll have to stop them.
Let's go!' ordered Dan. But Alfie and I didn't
budge. 'OOOh you are forgetting our treats!'
I woofed. So, Alfie and I sat up begging in a
pathetic way. 'Awww! all right you've earned
it,' chuckled Dan throwing us some meaty
chunks.
Alfie and I knew the drill. 'We are the leaders
now!' woofed Alfie proudly. The dark woods
looked ghostly against the backdrop of distant
gunfire. The sweet aroma of earth and summer
flowers mingled with the acrid smell of cordite.

Silently we moved forward, sniffing, stopping,
listening. Several times we had to lie flat - a
sign to take cover even though Dan and Jim
heard nothing. Progress was slow. Suddenly,
Alfie and I looked sideways and wagged our
tails, first slowly, then vigorously. 'A good
sign!' thought Dan - 'But what?'

'Shhh! I think I hear a dog whining!' whispered
Jim. We crouched low and crept forward. A
gust of wind whooshed through the giant oaks
and small bats darted silently through the trees.
Dan held his finger to his mouth to keep silent
as there was another distant sound of voices
blowing on the breeze. I pricked up my ears

and panted hotly. Alfie was on edge.

'I smell Tigger!' woofed Alfie. 'And I can hear Spam. She's in trouble!' I replied. We both yanked hard on our leads through the tangled undergrowth pulling Dan and Jim with us. Brambles scratched their hands as they cleared a path behind us.

We arrived at a small clearing. Jim gestured to Dan to stop us dogs immediately while he did his special fox call up into the tree canopy. Two frightened wood pigeons flew noisily from the trees. We all listened straining our ears. And then it came. Another fox call. It sounded quite close but Alfie and I knew exactly where it had come from yet didn't want to move. 'Something's not right,' whispered Jim looking at us dogs. 'Cover, take cover quickly!' ordered Dan. We all leapt out of the clearing back into the undergrowth and waited.

A long ten minutes passed. Then four German soldiers holding rifles staggered from the bushes into the clearing.

'HALT! Wer geht dahin?' (Who goes there?) Dan, Jim, Alfie and I stood rigid. We were all within firing range. One soldier cocked his gun and began to spin round in circles. 'Ha, ha, ha! Sie tanzen sehr gut Klaus!' said another soldier. But another shouted 'Schießen, schießen!' (shoot).

The spinning soldier raised his rifle to fire into the bushes. But at that moment a large animal flew through the air behind him and landed - SPLAT! straight on top of the soldier flattening him to the ground and snarling like a lion. It was Tigger! But.... BANG! the soldier fired his gun. It missed Tigger but hit his comrade in the foot.

'AHHHH!!! Dummkopf! sie schoß mein fuß!' yelled the angry soldier who was screaming with pain.

Shocked - the other soldiers grovelled in fear dropping their weapons. Harry, Tigger's handler jumped out pointing his gun at the terrified soldiers. Twigs snapped. Alfie and I hurtled from the bushes and pounced on the three other men. Dan and Jim kicked their guns away. Tied up and gagged they were taken prisoner while Dan radioed the platoon for back up. An hour later help arrived and the prisoners were marched away for interrogation, one on a stretcher.

CHAPTER FIVE

BEHIND ENEMY LINES

Harry's head hung down. He had bad news for the group. 'Spam jumped late and her parachute got tangled in a tree. Even worse, the Jerries shot at her and she's wounded. And Fred is missing. We must find them before the enemy,' he said darkly.

'It's dangerous. The enemy is everywhere. We need to spread out to find Fred and Spam, but stay within 'howling' distance in case we need help,' suggested Dan. 'And beware landmines. Let the dogs lead.'

Dan, Jim and Harry hugged each other and us dogs too - just in case they didn't see each other or us alive again. The men each had some cloths and socks of each others' scents for us dogs to sniff (not that we needed them!). After a while we split up and slowly moved forward.

Alfie was the first dog to lie flat - his warning of a landmine. He sniffed the air and ground to pick up tell-tale TNT trails. Jim marked the spot with a red cloth tie for the mine flail vehicle to detonate later. Alfie, Tigger and I detected 10 mines, so progress through the woods was slow and deadly.

Through the creeping dawn light, I moved forward, then stopped suddenly. My hackles went up.

'What's up boy?' asked Dan. He soon found out. 'I hear voices,' he whispered nervously. They were not speaking English. We crouched down to listen. Dan could see two German metal helmets only about twenty metres away. The soldiers were sitting in a trench, smoking and talking in low voices. Then Dan saw it.

'What the? Oh no! they've got a missile launcher' observed Dan. 'Well, the others aren't close, so we'll have to go for it alone boy. It's two of them against two of us! That launcher must be disabled.' I had to stay brave for Dan. 'I'm ready for action!' I told myself.

'They won't expect a big strong dog to leap on them,' Dan convinced himself as he made sure his rifle was loaded. But Dan hadn't expected the sneaky trick of dry twigs placed 15 metres all around the trench.

Suddenly - CRACK! the sound seemed to echo through the trees.The voices stopped and the

helmets sunk back into the trench. But not for
long.

The following five minutes held many
surprises. The missile launcher turned to face
Dan and me and the German soldiers swung
round with their rifles. But then Dan noticed
that I was missing and he was alone.

The soldiers didn't have time to turn at the
scuffling sound behind them as I flew through
the air and landed - PLONK - on top of them
knocking them down. They dropped their guns,
gasping in fear. Dan rushed in, but one soldier
was quick to recover his balance and snatched
his gun. He aimed it straight at me while I was
busy biting the other man. Dan jumped in to
protect me but in the scuffle the gun went off.
'Ahhhhh! Ahhhh!' I screamed. Then WHAM!
Dan was knocked unconscious and I couldn't
see at all. Everywhere was blackness.

Dan came round slowly. Five faces stared down
at him. 'We are outnumbered! ....outnumbered!
NO! NO!' he cried and sobbed like a child.
'Please, please save my dog. He's, he's …'

'Sshhh! Stay calm Monsieur. Nous sommes la

Résistance Française. Your dog will be all right, sir,' said one of the men in broken English. 'He has just passed out after a wound to his neck, but it is not serious Monsieur.'

Both German soldiers were tied up and led away and their weapons seized by the French.

Dan and I were carried to an underground hideout close by. 'Food and drink has never tasted so good! Thank you!' said Dan. I felt gentle hands soothing my injury and later lapped up a long drink of water.

'We must get going soon to find our friends,' explained Dan. 'Oh non, not yet,' replied Marcel, leader of the group. 'You must wait until you and your dog are better. Perhaps tomorrow night you go. One of our family will lead you in the right direction. But you must avoid the roads into villages as the Wehrmacht carry out spot-check controls and search people,' warned Marcel.

'Thank you very much for your kindness,' replied Dan. How can we ever repay you?' I woofed in agreement and waved a paw at Marcel. 'Ah - what an amazing dog you are

Buddy!' said Marcel tapping me on the head.
'Perhaps we will meet again one day when
France is free eh? Then we can share some fine
wine and food together - and laugh a lot!'

CHAPTER SIX

PRISONERS

Three miles away, Harry, Tigger, Jim and
Alfie trudged on through the woods, listening,
looking, sniffing the air for cordite or TNT.
Tigger and Alfie found four more landmines,
so reaching Spam and Fred was a slow and
dangerous process.
'I just hope our boys reach them first before the
enemy,' said Jim.

It was 7am and a blustery, cool summer's day.
The dogs sniffed the air and wagged their tails.
Alfie looked at Tigger. He had picked up the
same scent and sound. The dense woods fought
against them but they struggled on for another
two hours.
They pulled harder and harder on their leads.
Then Tigger ZOOMED forward. 'Slow down
Tigger!' commanded Harry, but he was not
listening. Even Alfie woofed a warning to
Tigger to stop, but that didn't work either.

Suddenly - BANG! a gun shot ricochet through
the trees scattering birds and forest animals. It
was very close. They were being shot at! 'Down,

get down!' shrieked Jim. Another shot clipped
a tree and whistled past. Even Tigger got the
message then and lay flat. He had certainly sniffed
out the enemy all right thought Jim.
'How many Jerries do you reckon there
are?' asked Harry hoping for a good answer
to his silly question, but Jim just shrugged.
'Don't know mate. Could be a few like us or
a hundred!' Harry shivered at the thought and
Tigger, being Tigger, licked Harry's face to
calm his master down.

In desperation, Jim cupped his hands over his
mouth and made a fox sound even though it
was not the right time of day. With guns loaded
and cocked they kept very still. 'We're hemmed
in I fear,' said Jim wiping the sweat from his
forehead. There was no fox call reply.

While Harry rummaged in his rucksack for
water he accidentally let go of Tigger's lead. It
was the chance Tigger had been waiting for.
'I need a diversion,' Tigger woofed softly to
his friend Alfie. 'Okay, but come back soon.
We need you,' responded Alfie with a puzzled
frown. But he trusted that Tigger had a good
plan.

First, Alfie chewed Jim's boot with great gusto - something he never ever did while it was still on his foot! Then, WHAM! he banged into Harry's back as he lay on the ground and started licking his face so that he couldn't see past Alfie's snout. 'Hey! what's up? Stop, hee! hee! you're tickling me Alfie.' And while Jim was trying to sort Alfie out as well, the two men didn't notice that Tigger had vanished.

Being a chocolate brown Labrador Tigger merged perfectly into the dried leaves still littering the forest floor and buried himself into the soft heaps of leaves. With quiet determination and extreme stealth he shuffled and crept like a large cat predator stalking its prey. But he faced a major problem. 'Serious back up, that's what I need before I attack!' he admitted.

Tigger sniffed and sniffed and wanted to leap in the air like he usually did when happy. 'Nope, better stay hidden for now, or I'll blow it!' he told himself. The scent of Fred and Spam were strong so they were close. But he could see something else; a Nazi camp of trenches and dens made of trees and twigs. 'OOOH Verdammt!' thought Tigger in his best German.

He slowly circled the camp undetected. There were about twenty Nazis. Five soldiers were on lookout duty - but their noses weren't up to much. 'Can't smell me like I can smell you!' Tigger thought proudly. But then his spirits wilted. The Nazi dens encircled a tree which had bits of parachute dangling from it and tied at the bottom of the tree was a man. It was Fred! Sitting closely at his side, bandaged up was his good friend - Spam.

CHAPTER SEVEN

TRACKING TIGGER

Tigger escapes

Harry, Jim and their German shepherd Alfie
had not moved from where Tigger had left
them, for fear of being shot, but knew they
had to do something. 'Where did Tigger go
Alfie?' whispered Harry. Alfie waved his paw
in the right direction and woofed softly, but
urgently. Then they knew. 'Right, you lead boy
- but carefully. We'll keep low and go slowly!'
whispered Harry patting Alfie's head.

Harry and Jim crouched and crawled like dogs themselves along the rough forest floor, responding to Alfie's warnings on the way. The canopy of ash, oaks and poplar trees kept them cool but the brambles and fallen twigs dug painfully into their bodies.

An hour later they arrived near the German Camp where Tigger was hiding. He bounced towards them wagging his tail in triumph of sniffing out the Germans. They slowly moved closer to the camp until they could see what was going on.

Harry and Jim hissed with rage at seeing Spam and Fred tied up under a tree. 'We have to plan the rescue carefully as we're definitely outnumbered!' admitted Jim. 'But how can we and two dogs attack twenty men with rifles and a missile launcher?' replied Harry. 'Er - Pray?' suggested Jim.

A few minutes later, Alfie and Tigger began to act strangely. They circled and sniffed around a small clearing behind them. Then started digging with their front paws. Their hackles were up and Tigger leapt about as if stung by a bee. They didn't dare bark as they knew they wouldn't get their treats. "Okay what's going on here?" puzzled Harry. Quite suddenly, the ground crumpled and moved- upwards! The cover of a tunnel shaft was being pushed up.

'Quick, hide!' ordered Jim as they crouched behind a bush. Both men aimed their rifles ready for the worst.
'Sssh! monsieur. We are the Resistance 'ere to 'elp you,' whispered a gentle female French voice. Jim and Harry were not convinced and didn't move. But when both dogs rushed to greet the emerging visitor, they knew it was a friend. 'If it's okay with the dogs - it's okay with me,' smiled Harry.

Very quietly they were led down into a hideout by Marianne where five men and two women had made a camp. They had a map of the whole area and knew exactly where the German trenches were. They even knew about Spam and Fred and explained their comrades had also seen Buddy and Dan.

'We have some big explosives,' said their leader Claud, 'but we have to rescue your friend first.' Both dogs woofed a reminder! 'Ah yes, and the dog of course!' he said stroking

Tigger's head. The others didn't want the explosion and more deaths but there was no other way. 'We have to theenk of the best way to do it,' said Marianne.

It was getting dark when Jim came up with a plan of how to rescue the hostages.
'I can be a moving bush and get close to cut their ropes. Listen, if it worked for the red indians in the westerns it will work for me now!' said Jim hopefully. 'There is a gap in their circle I can get through.' No one had any other ideas so it was agreed.

'And as soon as they are free, we shall blow up their camp,' added Claud.

It all sounded too simple to succeed and Harry was worried. 'Well, let me cover you as best I can,' he suggested. Half an hour later Jim's whole body was camouflaged with branches and twigs. 'You make a good bush. Just don't sneeze!' he smiled trying to calm Jim down.

The French got into position to charge. 'We will attack when Fred and Spam are free,' said Claud. 'The Germans are not expecting us so they won't be on their guard,' he added.

Down in the German trenches, the soldiers
were eating. Some climbed out and were
exercising their legs and arms. All their actions
showed they were not expecting trouble. They
were laughing and swearing and drinking wine
they had stolen from French vineyards.
'Excellent!' said Claud. 'Soon they will be
asleep and we can send in our bushman!'

But it took a long time as they were making
merry and talking not far from the tree. Spam
was agitated too as she smelled the others.
When she wagged her tail and stood up Claud
was really worried.

'You must go NOW Jim before they see the
dog!' Jim moved slowly along the ground so
that he looked like a heap of leaves. Fred had
seen him and sussed what was happening.
'Sshh Spam, sit girl - quiet!' And since she was
good at taking orders, she sat still, her eyes
fixed on Fred's face.
But just as Jim was about to cut the rope, a
German soldier staggered up from the trench
and shone a torch straight at the tree.
'Ahh, ha! Now shall I pee on you Tommy or Ihr
Hund eh?' Spam growled but Fred said nothing.
He just trembled in case Jim was discovered.

'Ha! ha!' screeched the soldier as he swayed about drunk, undid his flies and peed just where he stood.

Fred closed his eyes and said a prayer. The soldier crawled back into the trench and ten minutes later he was snoring.
Jim quickly cut through the ropes around Fred's wrists which were cold and bleeding. Slowly, Jim edged backwards through the gap followed by Fred and Spam. Immediately Claud and Marianne helped them into the tunnel where Tigger, Alfie and Harry were waiting and very excited to see them.
It was an emotional reunion, but cut short by Claud. 'Explosives - NOW!' he shouted. Everything was in place. The French had already spread the charges around the trenches and beneath the camp. Plus they had a supply of grenades.

'It is going to start a big fire!' said Marianne frowning. She did not like to kill these young men, but then remembered how they mercilessly shot down paratroopers falling, helpless, from aircraft. 'We 'ave no choice but to stop them,' she convinced herself.

CHAPTER EIGHT

BOOM!

Far across the forest on the other side, Dan and I left our other French Resistance friends. 'If you need us - we will know it!' said Marcel as he hugged me and Dan in a last farewell.

Dan looked me in the eye, 'It's time to find Spam and the others' he said. I whined and wagged my tail in agreement. Dan let me sniff Spam's scent cloth, even though I knew my friend's scent very well.

We set off when the sun dipped low on the horizon and fiery fingers of oranges and pinks spread across the sky. The forest buzzed with animal sounds. Crickets chirped and frogs croaked and their calls got louder as it got darker. Eventually Dan's eyes became accustomed to the blackness whereas my super sensitive night vision let me see things Dan couldn't.

Leaves crunched as we trudged through the forest, twigs snapped and tall poplars whispered. Far off, an owl hooted and the bark of a fox sailed on the breeze. Dan and I stood rigid at the same time. 'Was that the mating call of a real fox, or a call from one of the others?' whispered Dan.

Immediately he cupped his hands over his mouth and gave his best fox call up into the wind. Two minutes later it was answered. Three times he repeated the call and each time the answer got closer. I pulled on my lead towards the sound and - a familiar scent! 'Who is it boy?' asked Dan. 'Is it Harry or Jim?' Dan watched me in amazement as I nodded a 'yes' motion with my head. 'Well done boy, well done! Let's just stay behind this tree until they find us.'

But I sensed something else, something big was about to happen. I sniffed the air and trembled - DANGER! I reared up, grasped Dan around his neck and pushed him to the ground.

Moments later….. BOOM! A massive blast followed. The ground shook. Ammunition and missiles in the trenches exploded sending fire balls through the forest. Trees swayed and flared like Roman candles, catapulting daggers of wood through the air.

Dan and I lay hot and winded by the shock-wave that followed. The blast illuminated the sky and flames raged through the forest. I lay very still on top of Dan. He gasped for air, shaking and confused. Then, slowly reached up and stroked my head. 'You're so soft and silky Buddy,' he said quietly. But I felt nothing anymore.

'Hey boy! my best Buddy, my best Buddy, speak to me now, please. Don't leave me I need you, I need you…..' His words were muffled by sobs as he cried into the jet black softness of my chest. 'Dirty bastards! You'll pay for this.Oh, how you'll…pay! You'll pay swines!….. You'll pay!' He sobbed over and over uncontrollably.

Dan's sobs turned to choking as thick smoke swirled around. Twigs and branches crackled and spat in the intense heat. Dan tried to move but he had no feeling in his left leg. 'Guess we'll go together boy, just you and I.' A searing pain pierced Dan's head. He clasped his arms around my big body and talked of many things in his life before he fell silent. His body shuddered and lay still.

CHAPTER NINE

THE RESCUE

Nothing remained of the trenches. But miraculously five German soldiers survived and were taken prisoner. Two had shrapnel wounds, another had a broken arm and burns and the other two had bad cuts and burns to their arms.

After the blast, Jim, Harry, Fred and their dogs, Alfie, Tigger and Spam knew they had to find Dan and me as quickly as possible. The dogs sensed how close we were. They were agitated and raring to go. 'Let's hope they weren't caught in the blast!' said Jim with a worried frown.

The explosion was heard across many mlles by both the Nazis and our forces. Neither side knew who caused it or the number of casualties involved. It was 1a.m in the morning with no moon and still dark.The fire was spreading fast since it hadn't rained for three weeks and the breeze was strengthening.

'We must hurry to find them before we get cut off by the flames!' urged Harry. The dogs knew the safest route to escape but even their sense of smell was being challenged by the thick smoke. 'I shall try another fox call and hope Dan hears it,' said Jim hopefully. But after several calls and no response the situation became critical. 'We must wear our gas masks - and the dogs too - before we all pass out!' insisted Harry. It worked and they made faster progress through the acrid smoke.

Then, in unison, the three dogs scratched at their masks and whined trying to pull them off. 'Something is wrong. Perhaps they can't breathe!' said Jim. Once the masks were off, they pulled hard on their leads and woofed as loudly as they'd dare to - not breaking the 'no barking' rule.

With the fire closing in behind them, Harry shouted 'Release the dogs. If we don't make it, they probably will - and maybe get help!' Tigger leapt forward first and raced ahead with Alfie and Spam tagging behind. They disappeared into the smoke-filled darkness, woofing as they went so that the men could follow.

A gruelling, hot, ten minutes later, the men

found the dogs by a stream slurping thirstily
before they rushed on. They stopped at the base
of a giant oak tree panting and whining. Fred
spoke for the first time since his rescue. 'What
have they found - food perhaps?' But no, the
news was much better, or was it?
What looked like a heap of rumpled clothing
lay under a big black shape. The dogs jumped
on top, sniffed, licked and whined, then
pulled and burrowed into the heap. The men
approached cautiously. Was it a booby trap?
'Look! do you see it?' said Harry. Jim's heart
raced 'Oh yes!, yes I do. Quick! call off the
dogs!'

Something was sticking out of the heap. 'It's
one of our regulation army boots!' cried Fred. It
was a frightening sight. Dan's head was caked
with dried blood and his eyes were closed.
'It's Buddy! He's rigid and covering Dan.'
cried Harry. Very slowly the men lifted me
off. 'Buddy is still warm but has a very weak
heartbeat. I'll get some water from the stream,'
said Fred. My face was doused with cool water
which made me open my eyes. Soon Alfie and
Tigger were licking me too. 'He's just alive!
Keep him covered up,' said Harry.

Jim was caring for Dan but couldn't find a pulse. 'Let me try,' said Fred. 'And get some more water - quickly!' After a few minutes with no result, Fred started to give Dan CPR but his wrists were too weak after being tied up, so Harry took over, pumping his chest followed by the kiss of life.

He tried for ten minutes but then he cried out in desperation: 'Oh no, NO! This can't happen. Dan! Dan! come back Dan PLEASE matey. This can't be! No, it just can't be. He's gone. We've lost him! We've lost him!' he shouted, tears of sadness, confusion and anger rolling down his cheeks - as he finally pulled away in defeat and misery.

For some time we all sat very still listening to the crackle of burning trees screaming behind us, like our thoughts. No one spoke. After a while, Fred looked up to the sky and shouted something loudly. The others fell to their knees thumping the ground. The dogs whined and howled then sat by their masters offering their paws for comfort, but it was too late. Suddenly, Alfie and Tigger broke away and moved fast. They ran over and licked Dan's face and just wouldn't stop. But it was when

Tigger put his nose in Dan's ear that something extraordinary happened. Dan's head rolled to the side and his eyes shot open. 'He's alive! hooray! he's alive!' shouted Harry - and Tigger bounced a metre into the air.

In half an hour Dan was sitting up cuddling me. But part of his leg had been injured by wood shrapnel which meant he couldn't walk. 'If you hadn't pushed me to the ground Buddy, we would have died instantly from that blast. I'm so proud of you my clever, kind hero,' he said as he hugged me for a long time.
We all trudged on for another two hours pulling Dan on a make-shift stretcher. And then it began to rain - a light splatter at first, then a thundering downpour. 'At least this rain will stop the fire spreading,' said Fred cheerfully. 'Yeah, I think it's safe for us to make camp for the night,' suggested Harry. Everyone was relieved and thankful for the rest.

The next day, Tigger and I acted as messenger dogs. We delivered coded news to the Commanding Officer revealing where the German camps were. 'We'd better send both dogs in case one doesn't get through,' said Dan sorrowfully as he knew the Nazis were shooting dogs and pigeons on sight. But me being a black Lab and Tigger a brown Lab we had good camouflage in the forest.

Three days later there was still no sign of our platoon, but on the fourth day distant explosions meant the German camps had been found and destroyed. The day after that, as the moon's blue light crept eerily along the forest floor, a pair of fluorescent eyes of an animal bobbed about in the bushes. 'Mission completed!' woofed Tigger turning in circles trying to catch his tail.

But then Dan noticed Tigger was alone. He became very depressed and dared not think he would never see me again. After two days Dan feared the worst. He spoke little but cried lots.

In the dead of night on the third day under a moonless sky when the men and dogs were bivouacked by a river, a scuffling in the bushes woke the dogs. They scampered off to investigate. Half an hour later they returned. First they found Dan who was curled up in his one-man tent with his leg bandaged and up on a tree trunk. He was blowing his nose into his handkerchief.

'He's thinking of Buddy!' sussed Alfie. 'Let's surprise him and make him feel better.'

And so they did! I was waiting in the bushes until the dogs arrived. 'Dan needs you now. He's not well and is very sad,' woofed Spam. 'You must go to him right away!' Very slowly I crept into Dan's tent. His eyes were closed so I started to lick his face all over. Dan cried, smiled and laughed all at once and gave me the longest hug ever plus a special treat for coming back.

I then told them all about my special mission! 'After we delivered our messages, I was held back for a secret operation to check out a house they thought was booby trapped. My life was er, - disposable! It could have been the end of me!' I woofed shaking off the thought. 'I crept, listened and sniffed and knew the enemy was inside. So, I howled the alarm. Then the troops raided the house and captured the Nazis inside. They said I was a hero, but I just wanted to get back to Dan and all of you so they let me come back for more action! and here I am. So what's next guys?'

CHAPTER TEN

HOMEWARD BOUND

Dan's leg was getting worse and infected so it was time to get him back to base. 'If you go, we all go!' woofed Alfie. 'Definitely!' agreed Spam who just dreamt of lying in the sun on some cool grass. 'But we're 'The Fearless Four' - with more Nazis to catch!' woofed Tigger as he dived and splashed about in the river.

The next morning a naval dinghy floated upstream to pick us up and take us to a sea plane for our journey back to Britain.

Us dogs kissed and nuzzled each other in a big canine farewell, but each hoped it wasn't a last goodbye. Dan took me home to Sid, Ruth and Meira. I was so happy I raced around the garden at 40 mph until I couldn't run anymore, then lay on my back for one of Sid's special tummy tickles which I'd missed a lot. And for little Meira, I leapt high into the air and played ball. 'I'm HOME! home at last' I thought hardly able to believe it.

But all was not well with Spam. The War had

affected her more than she or her handler, Fred, had realised. When the army vet examined Spam he said she had suffered physically and mentally from her capture, probably due to being trapped in a tree with her parachute, being injured, shot at and then taken hostage by the Nazis.

'It won't be safe for her to live with her normal family again as she has developed unpredictable physiological problems - or post traumatic stress disorder. I'm afraid she must be put down,' he said in a - matter-of-fact sort of way. Fred cried. 'I can't let that happen, I just can't,' he sobbed. 'I promise to take care of her. My wife is dead and I have no children, so she can live with me,' explained Fred.
'I'll have to put it to the War Dogs Commission. We have to consider the safety of the public you know,' he replied coldly.

(Many War dogs were unable to return to normal life as they were considered a possible threat to humans because of their post traumatic stress disorder and had to be put down on their return home.)

None of the others knew about Spam until us dogs were reunited two weeks later. It happened at a prestigious awards ceremony in London for War dogs to receive their special service medals for outstanding bravery on the front line. On that day, Alfie, Tigger, Spam and I all received big shiny medals.

But late in the evening, we heard Fred explaining to Dan, Harry and Jim why the army wanted to put Spam down. We were very angry and sad. 'No! no! we shall rebel!' snarled Tigger. 'Spam needs help.' We all touched paws and made a pledge. 'We'll stand by Spam no matter what! and look after her always,' I woofed.

Letters were written to the authorities from Fred, Dan, Jim and Harry with back up from their Commanding Officer until eventually Spam was handed over officially to Fred. But Spam had to see the same vet every six months to check her condition.

It took over a year of tender care with walks in the country and by the sea and the closeness of us, her friends, for Spam to make a full recovery. But she was one of the lucky War dogs who lived on to enjoy her life.

Dan stayed close friends with Sid and our family so visited me often. We shared special times together with Tigger, Alfie and of course - Spam, even when the War ended. In fact, we stayed friends for life - as true friendship never dies.

Two years after the War, Sid became very ill and on the day he died, Dan and I together with Harry, Tigger, Jim, Alfie, Fred and Spam spent a wonderful night together under the stars like we used to in France. One star shone extra brightly that night. It seemed to move and zoom about in the vastness of space.

It's Sid my true friend and master - up there watching over us, I woofed proudly. The brightest star in the whole universe!"

THE END

The amazing Labrador

Black Labradors, along with golden retrievers and brown Labradors, originated in the Canadian province of Newfoundland and Labrador. They were originally named "St. John's dog" in tribute to the capital of Newfoundland.

It is believed Labradors were the result of cross-breeding between dogs such as spaniels, setters and the massive Newfoundland. Some records state that the St. John's dog and Labrador Retrievers evolved from various British and Portuguese breeds that were taken to Newfoundland in the 16th century. The powerful Newfoundland dog has the ability to swim long distances due to its huge lung capacity, webbed paws and thick oily and waterproof double coat.

Black Labradors are also renowned for their love of water - from a puddle to an ocean - and are often referred to as "water dogs" which probably has a genetic link to their powerful ancestor - the Newfoundland. In the 1700s, Labradors were in their element when fishermen in Newfoundland trained them to collect full nets and capture any fish that escaped.

In the 18th century black Labradors were the most popular bred colour until they were overtaken by the golden and brown variety. But later in the 19th century Newfoundland imposed high taxes on female dogs and families were restricted to owning just one dog. This nearly wiped out the breed which was heading for extinction - until 1991 when breeders in England restored the population.

Labradors are renowned for their accurate sense of smell which make them perfect as hunting dogs, even in waterlogged terrain. They are also skilled tracking dogs and can detect various substances, land mines, animals and humans even under fallen rubble which made them invaluable during the War years. Plus, their friendly, gentle nature make them ideal companions for those with special needs, or just as lovable pets.

Bod's Adventures

We know why Bod is so proud of his ancestor Buddy. But let's face it, he's done some pretty amazing things in his life too - so now it's time for his stories to be told.
For further details email: buddythewardog@gmail.com
Coming soon…………..

Danger for Crusty the crab
Bod has to make a big choice - does he save Crusty - or does he save himself?

Whispers in the waves
Something strange is happening at sea which Bod must investigate - fast! But it's a high risk situation.

Bod's scientific holiday
Bod is tracked down to help on a scientific expedition at sea after his cousin is injured. But the voyage has unpredictable consequences.

Deadly find
Fun and games on the beach until …..a treacherous situation arises.

Stowaway
A perilous adventure for Bod and his new unpredictable friend!

D-Day looms for Bod
Bod's future is at risk. A menacing threat lurks offshore which develops into a horrid, touch-and go situation.

Bod's Scottish holiday
Away from home, can Bod survive after his daredevil decision - to jump?